More Than Us

# More
# Than
# Us

Ryan Jones

ZENITH PUBLISHING

Supervising Editors: L. Austen Johnson, Caitlin Chrismon
Associate Editor(s): Isabel Barbi
Internal Formatting: Alexandria Boykin, Alma Basic
Cover Designer: L. Austen Johnson

GenZPublishing.org
Aberdeen, NJ
ISBN: 978-0-692-66284-7

*To the Butcher-Hagell family,*
*who have suffered the loss of a son and brother to suicide,*
*and to those who have experienced depression,*
*to those who keep fighting depression,*
*and to those who have lost people from depression—*
*you are not alone.*

## Warning

*This book contains the following: depression, anxiety, and suicide.*

If you or someone you know is suicidal, please reach out to the following mental health line:

**Phone: National Suicide Prevention Lifeline**
1-800-273-8255

**Online Chat:**
suicidepreventionlifeline.org

**A detailed list of mental health professionals can be found at:**
psychologytoday.com

1
—

*2008*

I was walking, you see, down an alley—I think it was a Friday night—when I stumbled upon something that would change my life forever.

I still remember how the feathers in my coat made a feeble effort to block the chill of the night. I still remember how the heat of my breath clouded the air with every rare exhale. It was so cold I had to remind myself to breathe.

I never knew taking the shortcut back to campus dorms after work would lead me to what my life is today, and I often wonder if I'd be the same person. If I never slipped on an invisible patch of ice, would I have seen him, or would the night have continued to swallow him, and possibly, taken his life?

I'll never know.

Because I did take the shortcut, and I did slip on ice, I did find him. The whole situation was an etch-a-sketch forever knobbed into my memory. When I slipped, all I could think was, *Damn, that'll leave a bruise.* And then, all it took was ten-seconds to look up and find his sallow face leaning against the dumpster, whiter than the bits of snow that clung to the metal. There was a knife, lying bloodied next to him, and the same bloodied patterns were painted on his wrists. And I remember screaming, or crying, or maybe both.

I called 911, rode in the ambulance with the dumpster boy, and told the paramedic exactly how I found him.

"If it wasn't for you, this boy may be dead by now," said the paramedic. I saved a life?

She glanced at me again, holding pressure on the boy's still-bleeding wrists. "What's your name?"

The question took me off guard. So simple, it didn't quite belong in this sickening scenario. "Lora," I said.

"Lora," she continued, "did you find any ID on him?"

"I didn't check," I croaked. I was too overwhelmed with the blood. My expression must have shifted as my thoughts went to the word "blood," because the paramedic spoke to me again.

"Lora, you going to be okay? It's all going to be all right."

My lips pressed into a paper-thin line. I nodded, fists clenching my knitted sweater, coat lying beside me, and I rumpled the fabric of the sweater into wooly balls. Knuckles white. Nostrils flared. It became difficult to breathe.

Even though the woman applied more pressure with endless gauze, crimson still managed to seep through.

"Ten minutes out," the driver cut, his voice slicing through a minimal opening between the front seats, competing with the beeps of machines and rumbles of the tires.

I remember not knowing that for the entire ride sirens were wailing. Yet they still echoed in my ears. Sometimes I remember this moment more vividly now than I did fifteen years ago, and it makes me think the subconscious has its own brain for memory.

What I can't remember is what the most startling moment was. Was it when the vehicle stopped without me realizing and doctors' claws started scratching through the newly opened back door? Or was it when one of their talons pegged me and dragged me from the rig and into the building? It also could have been the bustle of scrubs and sneakers and the rancid odour of age, death, and sickness all mixed into one scent—eau de hospital. I also can't remember where they took Dumpster Boy, but I remember a nurse leading me to a seating area, the pads of her fingers brushing my elbow, coaxing me into a puke-green seat. She sat next to me like she was an old friend and grabbed my hand.

"That's a very brave thing you did tonight. Most people would have up and run, but you didn't." I bit the inside of my lips because I didn't quite know what to say. "Here," the nurse said, handing me a plastic bag with her other hand. Inside was an unfamiliar wallet and phone. "These were in his pockets. If you decide you want to tuck it in for the night, just leave this at the nearest nurse's station." I nodded. "I would bring it myself, but I have a feeling you have some sort of tie to this boy, and that you'll be sticking around." She left with a final squeeze of my hand.

I remember checking my phone after placing the plastic bag on the chair next to me. I remember it being late, much too late, that if the next day weren't a weekend I wouldn't have stayed, but I did. Because it was the weekend and if I was the boy, I'd want someone to stay for me too.

## 2

The next morning, I woke up later than usual; the sun was already cutting across the floor from whole-walled windows, and doctors were already holding morning coffees. I checked my phone and was dragged back by last night's encounter from the hole I tried to shove it down.

As I walked to the nurses' station, the Ziplock bag clung to my clammy hands, and my nerves were sparklers spewing in all directions. The nurse behind the desk was topped with a blonde perm and rosy cheeks.

I cleared my throat. "Excuse me." Nothing. She didn't flinch—she just continued to stare into the illuminated screen. "Excuse me," I tried again, and this time her rouge cheeks perked. Her eyes narrowed, and she gave me a good once-over.

"Can I help you?"

"Actually, I think you can," I began, "or I hope you can. You see, I came in here last night with a boy who... with a boy who..."

"You need to be a little clearer, dear." She started twirling her hair, and I was afraid she was growing bored. I just couldn't bring myself to say the words, *with a boy who cut himself.*

A familiar voice saved me. "You stayed all night?" It's the nurse who sat next to me. "Don't you have any place to be?"

"It's the weekend," I replied, "so I don't have any classes. Also, I'd like to know how he's—how the boy is doing. Is he okay?"

She set a fist on her hip and leaned into it with a smile. "Since no family has come to claim him, and we can't find any relatives, I'm sure a warm presence will benefit him. Come."

At the last word of her sentence, she'd already started on the way from whence she had come. My feet finally remembered their purpose and followed her. My phone buzzed in my pocket as we reached silver elevator doors.

"How old are you anyway, Lora?"

"Twenty."

"A student?" she asked.

"Yes," I replied.

"About the age of my own son. If you two had switched places last night, I'd like to think he would have done the same as you."

I offered a smile and replied in my mind, if *he's anything like you I'm sure he would have*. When the elevator opened, we were sardines packed inside a can, and I hoped we didn't have many levels to travel because I was claustrophobic. The majority of the buttons were already lit from pressing fingers, so when we reached level four and the nurse broke away from the crowd, I was thankful to be able to breathe again. As my feet shuffled across the linoleum, unsure of where the path led, a sign greeted my face reading: "Psychology." The rectangle of plastic looked like it was trapping each of the letters just like every patient that was trapped in a bed inside a room.

We turned left and headed down a hallway that ended with another large window and made a right into a room. I caught the number from my peripheral: 402.

My feet almost stopped working—yet again—upon entry of the room, as if the line of the door frame was a safe zone between thought and reality. Thoughts could roam my mind, and eventually they'd get tired and sit down, but reality has nowhere to roam when it's the most real of the things staring you in the eye.

The nurse checked his vitals (or what I assumed were vitals), glancing at the levels on the machine and jostling with the IV. She pulled the sheet higher over the boy's chest. He didn't move.

"He's in an induced coma right now," she said. "The doctors thought it would do him some good, give him some much-needed sleep." She checked the tape that secured his IV line. "You can take a seat if you'd like," she said, pointing to a chair facing the right side of the bed.

I didn't know what else to do, so I brought myself to the chair. The brown cushion was much too firm and it forced me to sit upright.

"Here," she said, walking over to me, "I'll take that."

For a second I was confused about what she was referring to until she took the Ziplock bag from my grasp and gave it a spot on the bedside table.

"We'll give it to him when he wakes up or when the doctors decide it's best." She folded the plastic lip under the contents, securing the two objects. "If you ever decide to make regular visits or if you ever need anything, just ask for Maggie, and I'll come running."

"Thank you," I said. Maggie was about to leave, but a question kept poking the center of my forehead. "Maggie?"

"Yes, dear?" She turned back around.

"How could—I mean, why has no one come for him yet?"

A frown sank her face, an anchor embedding itself in the seabed for the ship to rest, and her brows crinkled in worrisome waves. "Not everyone has someone who loves them."

**3**

———

Having no one in your life who loves you must be an awful thing. And it was this very thought, this disturbing hint of a stranger's reality, that made me stay until dinnertime. I'll admit, at first it was rather awkward. Sometimes it felt as if I were talking to myself or an imaginary friend.

"I hope you're having sweet dreams at least," I'd say. "At least you're catching up on some beauty sleep."

Around lunchtime, I made my way to the cafeteria and purchased a tuna sandwich and a cup of green tea. I brought the food to a table and took a seat. I unraveled the cling wrap from the sandwich and took the first bite, lettuce crunching between my teeth.

I glanced around and noticed that half the tables were empty. Not everyone must like eating lunch in a hospital cafeteria. I couldn't imagine why. But what I also noticed about the half of the tables that *were* occupied was that they were also empty with only one person sitting at each, much like myself. An old man stared into the black hole of a coffee cup. A middle-aged woman, gray strands mixing brown, poked at a salad. All the while, a little girl stood beside her, tapping her arm, wanting her to, "Please look at my doll."

Sadness makes humans a lonely species—sadness and hurt. And all I can remember was how completely alone I felt in that cafeteria and how incredibly alone the boy must have felt to put himself in such a situation.

I finished my tuna sandwich, the bites like sand in my mouth, tasteless and gritty. I discarded the saran wrap in the trash and took the elevator back up to level four, tea in hand. It offered warmth through the Styrofoam, but it failed to make me feel better, even a little bit. I entered room 402 again and made small talk with myself and the imagined version of Dumpster Boy I had in my mind for another while.

"Do you like tea? I have a feeling you'd like tea," I said. "I bet your favourite is chai, or maybe some type of rooibos."

"You know, some people think that when people are in comas they can see themselves because they're floating ghosts in the room." I glanced around the room to make sure nothing had moved.

After a little bit, I said, "I wonder if you can hear me. I'm sorry if you can and if you don't want me here, but being alone is quite awful."

By the time I'd finished speaking out loud, I felt my mind melting. I felt as if I were going crazy. I stood up and shrugged my coat over my shoulders.

"I'll be back tomorrow after my shift. It won't be all day, but at least it's something."

Before I left the room, I stared at his sleeping face, wondering what his voice would sound like: baritone or tenor, smooth or gravelly? I also wondered what his name may be and how tall he'd stand. When I grew tired of the guessing game, I rode the elevator down to ground level and walked to the closest bus stop. I

9

didn't feel like walking because the last time I did, I found myself at a hospital with a stranger. Now, I found myself seated on a heated bus next to a snoring, balding man—my company for the entire ride to the dorms.

## 4

There are two types of bus drivers in this world: those who don't know and don't care about you no matter how many times you ride their route, and those who keep your face and stops in memory.

The old man's snoring must have lulled me to sleep because I was woken up by the driver's voice.

"Lora. Lora, this is your stop."

My eyes fluttered open as the world took shape, a crowd of strangers wearing winter coats. Jimmie, the driver, had turned out of his seat to face me.

"Oh, jeez. Thanks, Jimmie," I said, making sure I had all my belongings accounted for. "Sorry for the holdup."

"Don't mention it," he said as I walked past him, "but make sure to get some sleep."

The bus roared as Jimmie hit the gas, and I was left alone on campus under the lantern lights. Only one or two other students milled about on a Saturday evening, most likely heading to visit family or bustling to study at the nearest cafe. I glanced down at my phone and caught my reflection. Chills shook my body.

On my journey back from the hospital, the sun had disappeared. I clicked the home button only to see my screen filled with texts and missed calls from Deirdre, my roommate:

*Deirdre: Lora, where are you? You never stay out. Please get back to me.*

*Deirde: Lora, I'm starting to get rather worried about you. Call me.*

*Deirdre: That's it. If you're not back by the end of the night I'm calling the cops and filing a missing person's report.*

Given the situation, the notion was shoved so far back in my mind. I dragged my feet across the rubber mat and swiped my student card to gain access to the building and its heat. I pressed the upward arrow on the elevator, and once inside, pressed number four, wishing that Deirdre wouldn't be completely pissed (she was). I didn't even have to sift my key from the bottom of my coat pocket; she was already waiting for me—deep-set frown, scowl, our door thrown wide open as she stood, glaring at me in the hallway.

"I was this close," she said, pinching her thumb and forefinger together, "this close to calling the cops."

"Hi, Deirdre."

I shuffled past her into the room. I discarded my coat on the bench next to the closet.

"Hang that up," Deirdre demanded.

I'd never made her so mad before and did as she said, cringing at the whine of the closet's hinge as I opened and closed the door.

"Not a call. Not even a single text. I was worried sick. I thought something happened to you. I thought you were hurt—or worse, kidnapped."

"None of the above," I said, plopping down on my bed, head leaning against the wall.

"Then where the hell were you? What happened?"

I didn't know how to go about explaining last night's endeavor, but my silence only made her more furious, and her tone of voice was nails on a chalkboard.

"Lora?"

I glanced up at her, placing my hands underneath my legs, as if doing so would offer me an extra inch of support.

"I saved a boy from dying," I said.

At this point, Deirdre looked like she was fighting against hysterics.

"Come again?"

I repeated myself. "I saved a boy from dying."

"What on earth... Is this a joke?"

"No," I said.

I told her to take a seat and then unleashed the whole story. How I fell on ice walking back after work, how I found his limp body. How my lungs pressed tightly together in fear, how I couldn't breathe.

"But I called 911, and he got the help he needed," I said. "I'm sorry I didn't call or text. My mind was completely consumed in the moment. I stayed with him at the hospital because he had no one."

"Oh...wow...okay," Deirdre said. She got off her bed and gripped me in a hug.

**5**
———

Before leaving for my shift at the campus cafe I reminded Deirdre that I wouldn't be back right after because I'd be stopping by the hospital to visit. The darkness outside beckoned me to remain quiet for the sleeping.

"No problem," she said, "just don't make it too much of a habit waking me up at the crack of dawn."

I laughed to myself at her dramatics. I often forgot that not everyone was a morning person. I had no choice in the matter because the boss opened shop at 7:30 a.m. I never minded the morning shifts—it left me to do what I wished for the rest of the day, including visiting the boy.

Two employees were required to complete the opening tasks, and I found March already cleaning dishes in the backroom from an early start on prep.

"'Morning, Marchie," I said, hanging my coat on the rack. I stepped on a chair and switched the heater on above the door.

"What's shaking, Lora?" she asked, popping her head from behind the counter.

No matter which way she moved, her dark curls always bounced and her eyes were always framed by her obnoxiously round glasses, a beaded string attached to either leg so she could wear the spectacles as a necklace.

"Not too much," I replied.

I joined her around the counter and plucked my full-body apron from its named-peg in the backroom. Mine still had a frothy milk-stain from last night when I spilt a cappuccino, and last night was also when…

I stopped my mind from wandering by plucking a marker from a glass jar, uncapping it to reveal a fluorescent green. Taking a wet cloth and a step ladder from the backroom, I wiped away yesterday's menu options and made the additions for today. Once complete, I circled the counter to kneel in front of the wooden stand and advertise the drink of the day.

"What'll it be, Marchie?"

"Apple-spiced cappuccino," she said, wiping the overhang of the granite countertop above me. "Here," she said.

I heard the plunk of something on the counter. I stand up to notice that Marchie has placed a paper cup full of frothy, caramel coloured liquid.

"Try it. Tell me what you think."

I took a hesitant sip, but then downed two more grateful ones, my tongue tingling.

"How do you think of these things?"

She wore a proud grin on her face. "I don't know, the stuff runs in my veins. It hits me over night."

I shook my head in disbelief.

I turned on the open sign and then started to count the till. The clinking of coins almost drowned out her voice, but I heard her next question. "Are you okay with manning the till today?"

"Of course," I said.

Once I inputted the numbers into the system, the first customer moseyed his way in: Gregory, a music major. I only knew this because he carried his acoustic guitar everywhere he went, and he came in for green tea every Sunday morning before practice. I'd gotten to know a bit of his life story.

"The usual?" I asked.

"You know it," he said. A smile warmed his wind-burned cheeks. "Though, could you also add a blueberry muffin to that? I'm running late this morning and didn't get a chance to eat breakfast."

"Sure thing. Get that, Marchie?"

She nodded. The teabag was already hanging over the lid of the cup as the kettle began to steam and she'd already packed his muffin inside a paper bag.

"Have a good day, Greg," I said, handing him his contents.

"You too, Lora."

I glanced over my shoulder to see if Marchie was too busy. She wasn't. "It's people like that who make this job worthwhile."

Usually, my shifts were rather speedy, consisting of serving latte after espresso after cappuccino, but this day dragged. People say time slows down when you're anticipating something. But was I really anticipating? Too many lattes. Too many espressos. Too many cappuccinos.

Eventually, the rush slowed and the sun rose to its place in the sky, signaling afternoon had arrived. Malcolm came in for his afternoon shift, and I was relieved of duty. Before untying my apron, I put a sandwich together and packed a bag of cookies on the side.

"You going somewhere?" asked Marchie. I've never prepared food for myself after a shift.

"Mhm," I replied. "I'm visiting a friend."

I didn't have to see Malcolm's face to know that he was wiggling his eyebrows in a flirtatious manner. "A boyfriend?" he jested.

I rolled my eyes. "Not in the slightest."

Marchie grabbed a tea towel off the counter and wound it up, spinning it in a dozen circles—a fabric helicopter—only to flick her wrist and crack Malcolm across the back. His mouth opened in question but held back laughter all the same, he spun around.

Marchie pointed a finger in his face and she got so close that I thought she was going to pick his nose. "You leave her alone. Stop bugging her."

By that time, I had already discarded my apron and slipped into my coat. Chills crept over my body, reminding me of last night's events. I hoisted my purse over my shoulder and held the paper-bag lunch in my hand.

"See you tomorrow, Marchie. Malcolm." I nodded my head at him, an acknowledgment of understanding. He just liked to tease.

"Have a good one," called Marchie as I was halfway out the door.

"I'll try."

But there was no particular good about where I was going and what I was doing.

6
———

I was wishing and hoping—wishing and hoping damn hard—that some type of obstacle would have blundered my path and made it impossible to get to the hospital. A flat tire, perhaps. Or maybe, the bus itself would break down. But Deirdre taught me that wishes are empty words and thoughts—empty words and thoughts that are useless. I could wish on every peak of every star, and all the wishes and peaks wouldn't make a difference because they'd never come true.

I wasn't being awful: I was just being human, and I was terrified of the possibility that this time the boy would be upright in bed chatting away, or he would be upright in bed and remain quiet as a mouse. Whichever he preferred. But both of these possibilities petrified me, and I almost didn't get off the bus when the vehicle jerked to a stop. It felt as though the blood in my legs had been replaced with liquid cement and each step was excruciating, but I made it off the bus, the hospital within eyesight.

The sliding doors closed behind me in a hurry. My feet remembered the path and brought me to the main elevator in the lobby.

Upward button. Doors open. Doors close. Level four.

Almost no one was occupying the elevator this time, but at that moment, I wished for nothing more than the presence of a dozen other bodies. Feeling like a squashed sardine would beat the feeling of a lonesome astronaut floating in space.

My breath hitched when the doors parted and "Psychology" welcomed me once again.

The hallway leading to his room was a runway but not the glamorous type. Although it contained the same unruly distance, it lacked excitement. Cameras were replaced with sanitizer dispensers lining the walls and flashes of light were mocked by the buzzing of the overhead, fluorescent bulbs.

I walked into his room with a lump clogging my airway, but as soon as I saw him, the lump dissolved, and I could breathe again. He was still asleep.

Where I thought I'd find relief was packed with worry. Why hadn't the doctors woken him yet? Isn't he ready? It's been two days, or two nights rather. I didn't realize I was blocking the doorway until a white lab coat brushed my arm and blinded my peripherals.

"Excuse me," a male voice grunted. For a second, I thought he was drifting a pen back and forth in front of the boy's face when I realized it was just a tiny flashlight. He opened each eyelid and shot a beam into his pupils. I just stood and stared—frozen.

"Excuse me." The man cleared his throat and his dark features exuded intimidation. "Are you supposed to be here?" he asked. "Are you family?"

*I'm the only person he has*, I wanted to say, but didn't.

"I'm going to call security."

I focused on his name tag: Dr. Preston. He rushed past me again, but I stopped him at the door.

"Maggie," I stuttered. "She's a nurse here. She told me it was okay to stay because he has nobody. I'm the one who found him."

His crescent-slitted eyes expanded into full moons at a rate that would shock any astronomer. He didn't leave me with words, but he left me wondering with questions.

7
——

From how the interaction began to how it ended, I was certain I'd be in the worst of trouble, or the worst up to that point in my life. Images of security dragging me from the building played over and over in my mind as I took residence in the uncomfortable chair.

I took my coat off and hung it on the back of the leather, claiming my territory. I didn't want to leave, nor should I have to. I tried blocking out raised voices that started spilling over from the hallway, but it didn't work. The voices grew louder and inched closer until they were right in the room: Dr. Preston and Maggie. I almost wanted to pull up a stiff chair for them to sit down in to lighten the weight of tension.

"Dr. Preston. Leniency, if you will," said Maggie. "I know all about hospital protocols. I know about its rules and regulations. But you know just as well as I do that sometimes these rules and regulations don't apply to certain situations."

Dr. Preston crossed his arms and tilted his head toward me. "She's not family, Maggie."

"So, when that boy wakes up and has no one, you think that will be much better?"

Dr. Preston tucked his lips in, pressing the skin together until the pink turned white. I was grateful for Maggie and her determination; because of her, I was able to stay.

"Fine. But if her being here is more of a hindrance than a benefit, she's gone."

Maggie nodded in agreement and when Dr. Preston left the room, tension followed his trail. Maggie walked to my side and offered a one-armed hug.

"I expected him to be awake," I said, looking up at her, searching her face for an ounce of hope. I've never seen age look so dignified on anyone besides my own mom.

"I thought he would be too, but the doctors thought it best to give him a little more time. The damage is more than skin deep."

"Of course, that makes sense."

"How long are you sticking around today?" Maggie asked.

"I'm not entirely sure. I have classes all day tomorrow, so it can't be too late."

"Don't wear yourself thin. Only visit when possible."

She squeezed my shoulder then left the room. She has other patients to tend to. The Ziplock bag is still tucked into its spot on the bedside table. I probably shouldn't have done what I did, but I did it anyway.

Carefully and gently, as if the walls had eyes, I brought the plastic bag onto my lap. I peeled apart the seams, which made a zipper sound. I didn't know if what I was doing was illegal or if it was breaking some sort of policy. All I knew was that it was wrong to go through a person's belongings when they're lying in a hospital bed right in front of you.

I checked his phone first. When I pressed the home button, the screen remained black, so I held down the little rectangle on the side of the device. A low battery icon popped up.

I then plucked the wallet out of the plastic and opened the black leather to find a few ten-dollar bills and a driver's license.

Name: Engels / Harper, Lee

I skipped over his address because I'm not that much of a sleuth. Beside the word AGE sat two numbers: 22.

Harper Lee Engles. 22.

I could put a name to the face. I looked up and took a deep breath, holding it for a few moments as I traced his sleeping features with my eyes.

*I'm sorry you've done this to yourself Harper... I am here.*

8
———

I unwrapped the bagel and scarfed it down, the tiny sesame seeds scratching my dry throat. I should have brought some water— a useless afterthought.

I didn't stay too long afterward due to school and work the next day, but a couple hours sufficed. I also didn't want Deirdre worrying about me, so I texted her when I was on my way back to campus.

Thirty minutes later, the bus deposited me near the dorms and from there it was a ten-minute walk—only the walk felt like twenty. Despite the setting sun, the breeze bit, leaving my skin burning red and raw. I reminded myself to apply lotion once I got in the room.

I brushed my feet against the mat, swiped my card, then hit the "up" button embedded in the panel next to the elevator. All I wanted to do was take off my boots, slide into pajamas, and catch up on some English readings. Those plans, aside from the boots, were placed on a back burner because something more delicious wafted from the oven—grease, cheese and spices of pepperoni. My fingers tingled. My mouth watered. I thought my tongue was going to drown.

"Hello," said Deirdre. Her face was glowing, and it reflected in the open laptop, playing a show. Beside her, resting on a TV tray, lay a white cardboard box with red lettering.

"I hope you don't mind," said Deirdre. "I ordered some pizza. Queen-sized. I thought you might like some."

"Thank you." The bagel didn't make a dent in my hunger, merely a tide-over.

I grabbed a sweatshirt and jogging pants from my dresser. "Just going to change."

I heard corny laughter floating from the laptop speaker through the bathroom door, the fake type producers use with intention because they think that adding the sound effect will make the viewers laugh too. It works sometimes, I suppose, but in general it's just annoying.

Deirdre sidled over, making room for me on her bed, and handed me a paper plate with two slices of cover pieces—my favourite. I found a seat on the comforter and was met with the faces of Chandler and Ross.

"Do you ever watch a different show, aside from *Friends*?"

"Of course not. Then you'd think there was something wrong with me."

We ate in the company of the dysfunctional group, but once the episode was finished, and all that was left were lonely crusts, she closed the laptop.

"So," Deirdre began, "you want to talk about it?"

My fingers were pressed against the paper plate, needing to be occupied. The spotlight isn't my thing, even with an audience of one.

"Talk about what?" I hoped that if I played dumb she'd move on.

"Lora..." Her voice dropped off. She caught me.

"There's nothing really to talk about."

"Are you certain?" asked Deirdre. "No post-traumatic stress?"

"Nope." I shook my head. "I feel fine."

"I see," she said. Her eyes were shovels digging holes in the side of my face. "Did you go visit him today?"

"I did."

"And?"

"He's still in an induced coma."

Rising and falling, her shoulders reminded me of a hang glider, floating on the currents of a sigh. "Lora, I don't want you to get your hopes up."

"Deirdre, the coma is induced. His brain is fine." My statement was false, I realized. "Or sort of fine." *But we're all messed up.*

"Do you really think it's the healthiest option—becoming invested in him?" Deirdre was two years older and often treated me like I was her little sister, but I wasn't. "I mean he got himself in this situation because something wasn't right. When he wakes up, or if, I don't want it to affect you or change you."

"My gosh," I scoffed. "Do you actually hear yourself?" I untangled myself from crisscross and flung my plate inside the pizza box, standing up and turning around for a moment to catch a breath. "Depression isn't some virus you *catch* from breathing contaminated air, from being exposed to coughs and sneezes. It's a serious disease of self-worthlessness—a disease without a definite cure. But it's not

26

contagious, and I won't become tainted. He needs help, not people like you who think depressed people should remain isolated."

I don't know when the atmosphere shifted, or how or why, but it did. Long gone was the warmth of oven-baked dough and the fake laughter was now a distant memory, as if it never existed.

Deirdre's words were icicles, the type that looked like they could fall from the rooftop at any minute, so you shouldn't stand too close. "I think we're done here."

She didn't bother to clean up the pizza or put away the TV tray, she just pulled down her covers in a flurry, burrowed somewhere deep inside, and shut off the lamp.

She left me standing in the dark.

## 9

No one understood why I felt the need to be there for Harper, and I think it's because people lacked knowledge of my background. Everyone carries their own backpacks. Inside my backpack, people would find out why my parents called almost every night at school, asking me about my day and how work is going. They'd want to know every detail each time, from the type of homework assigned to the clothes I wore that day. People would think they were crazy, if they untied my knapsack and discovered all its contents, but I knew they were just parents, parents who loved their daughter with hurting hearts.

Sleepless nights were never my friend. Those were the nights when the past would creep up from behind and tap me on the shoulder, nodding the brim of its fedora in salute. I don't acknowledge. I don't wave. I just let it happen—the remembering.

I wasn't always an only child.

Over a year ago, I used to have a brother. Blonde hair, like mine, and he always wore the largest smile. He had us fooled.

It was my last year of high school, senior year, the very beginning when teachers introduce lessons and implement classroom rules such as NO USE OF PHONES.

It was in one of those classrooms that my phone started vibrating. I automatically hit the button on my phone to cease the noise, hoping my math teacher, Mr. Carter, didn't pick up on the call. He has hound ears.

"Do you need to leave the room, Lora?" he asked.

My phone buzzed again. I looked down and found my mom's face filling the screen. Again, I declined.

"Sorry, Mr. Carter."

"No phones in class people."

He turned back to the blackboard to continue writing an unfinished question, but my phone buzzed another time.

"Lora."

I was going to be in trouble, but I wiggled out of my desk and hurried into the hallway. I walked a few paces down the hall and leaned against the black and white lockers. They were cold. I picked up.

"Mom, you know I'm in class..."

"Lora." Her voice broke. "Something has happened."

My brother was overall talented: good grades, played on the football team, and even worked with the drama club.

He told my mom that morning that he wasn't feeling too well, so he was able to stay home. When she went to check on him during her lunch break, the house was silent.

"William?"

Quiet.

"William?"

She called again and again from the foyer and tried again several more times as she climbed up the stairs.

But William would never answer because he was fast asleep, a whole bottle of pills bloating his stomach.

## 10

That was one of the first nights in university that I didn't sleep well. Memory after memory replayed and just when I thought the loop would end, it would play again. I remember I glanced at my clock and read 4 a.m. Two hours later, my alarm rang and my hand came smashing down on top of the electronic.

*I'll need a lot of coffee today*, I told myself.

I rolled over onto my left side and saw that Deirdre's bed was empty. I got changed, brushed my teeth, fixed my hair, and grabbed my school bag from the bench it was sitting atop at the foot of my bed.

*On with the day*, I told myself. *Two hours of sleep or not.*

I stopped by the campus cafe before Workshop.

"Hi, Marchie."

"Hi, sweetheart." I removed my hat so I could hear better.

"What can I get you?"

"A large mocha with two shots of espresso, please."

Her whole body jerked.

"Two shots," she repeated. "Did I hear right?"

"Unfortunately so."

Dishes clanked and machines whirred as the metal arm spun round and round inside the silver canister. I almost didn't hear her next words over the cacophony.

"Deirdre keep you up?"

"No." I shook my head. "Just couldn't sleep."

My ears rang from the clamour, even when the shop was quiet again and all I could hear was the pop of a lid being pressed onto a to-go cup. She slid the drink across the counter.

"Thanks, Marchie."

"Have yourself a good one."

I fixed my hat back into place. The walk to class wasn't too long, but again, winter bared its presence.

I entered the building and stomped down the stairs to the basement where the lecture hall was located, leaving a trail of snow chunks. Class didn't start for another twenty minutes, and people were still turned around in their chairs, talking to one another. I found my spot next to my classmate Ophelia and placed my bag on the chair next to me. She was typing away, black letters filling the not-so-empty white space.

"How does this sound?" she asked, spinning her laptop in my direction. I hadn't even sat down yet, barely had time to place my coffee on the table and was still attempting to undress. I fumbled with my scarf as I read the sentence she was pointing to.

"That sounds great, but I'd add a comma there," I pointed.

"Hmmm. That actually may work."

I discarded my mittens, took off my hat, unzipped my coat and settled into the cushioned seat.

*The hospital should have chairs like these*, I thought.

After taking a sip from the paper cup, I took my laptop out of my bag and placed it on the table, opening it up. I typed in my passcode and quickly opened the document for one of my WIPs.

"What are you bringing to the workshop today?" asked Ophelia.

I spoke with honesty, "I'm not really sure. Maybe the next chapters I wrote for my romance novel."

Mr. Murphy walked into the room and chatter no longer filled the odd empty seat.

The workshop went smooth, and for the rest of the class, Mr. Murphy asked us to work on rewrites, incorporating the advice and critiques of our peers. I was about to begin when I received a text message.

*Mom: YOUR FATHER AND I ARE TAKING YOU OUT FOR DINNER TONIGHT. SEE YOU AT SIX.*

This single text threw a wrench in my plans and left me wondering how I was going to slot time to go to the hospital.

## 11

I didn't have time.

By the time Editing and Publication finished, I was already an hour late to the restaurant. I also had to drop off my backpack in the dorm. Deirdre's bed was still unmade—she'd yet to pop in.

When I did make it to the restaurant, my parents were delighted. Mom squeezed me in her arms.

"Oh, Lora, it feels like it's been ages since I've seen you," she said.

I muffled a choke through my curtain of hair. She doesn't know the ramifications of her strength.

"It's been three months," I said.

"Three months too long," said Dad, sliding me into a one-armed embrace.

"Well, sit, sit," Mom fussed. "I hope you don't mind," she said tucking one side of her grey bob behind her ear, "but we ordered breadsticks to start."

"Sounds perfect," I replied. I shrugged my coat from my shoulders and draped it on the back of the empty chair. My parents had already piled theirs on top.

"It's awfully brisk," Dad said. Often, too often, he'd use weather to break into conversation.

"Well, it is winter," I replied. "How's work?"

"It's going great." Dad took his glasses from his shirt pocket and placed them on his nose so he could read the beverage menu. "Making lots of money with people needing winter tires. Dear, would you like a glass of wine?" He turned to Mom.

"No, it's quite all right," she replied, raising her glass. "I'll stick with my water."

"And what about you, Mom? How's work?" I asked again.

"It's fine, though the office is always terribly cold. I believe they keep the AC on year-long." She took a sip of water. "Flu shots have been popular. Have you thought about getting one this year?"

I told her what I said every year: "No, Mom, I don't believe in them."

Dad chuckled like he usually does, and the waiter dropped off the basket of breadsticks. Each of us plucked one from the plastic. Dad buttered his, but Mom and I broke ours into bite-sized pieces. When Dad finished his, he wiped the grease off the tips of fingers using the napkin he'd folded on top of his lap. He then moved to brush crumbs from his mouth.

"So, Lora," he began. I looked up mid-bite, the dough melting on my tongue. "Your mother and I have some news to share with you."

"Oh," I managed through the clump of bread that rolled down my throat. Did they get a new car? Is one of them retiring? Is Mom going to start dying her hair? Is she...?

"Are you pregnant?" I blurted, eyes bulging towards Mom.

She brought a fist to cover her mouth and coughed several times. Dad wiggled his fingers around the collar of his shirt, attempting to create more space.

"Goodness, no," Mom said. "I'm much too old for that."

"Then, what is it?"

"We're selling the house," Dad said. "We'll still be in Niagara, but we found a beautiful house on the lake made entirely of wood. It feels more like a cabin so it'll feel like you're camping all the time."

"But why?" I asked.

I was furious. That house that was nested in the curve of Burberry Court (812) had been the only home I'd ever known—it was *my* home. It was where notches were grooved into my bedroom door frame, measuring how tall I'd grow each month. I never got a growth spurt. It was a steady climb. It's where I coloured the living room walls with purple crayon. Boy, was Mom upset. It's where I learned to ride a bike. It's where I studied for all my high school exams and took prom photos with friends.

A person can't just move buildings and label the walls, windows and doors "home." Home isn't a building; it's memories. Even if some of the memories hurt.

"Is this because of William?" I asked. "That's why you're doing this, isn't it?"

Mom was tight-lipped and Dad stared at the table.

"We think it would be good, a fresh start," said Dad. "Don't you think?"

My heart broke that evening. I never considered that my parents would make such a decision—moving to a place, no room for William.

"What about his things?"

Mom cleared her throat. "Some of it we'll pack and take with us; the rest, we'll donate."

We left his room untouched, trying to conserve as much of his existence as possible.

"When?" I asked.

"At the end of the month," replied Dad.

"We wanted to be able to celebrate Christmas at the new place," said Mom.

It was difficult to order food, let alone eat it once it arrived. I didn't taste it, just felt it on my tongue and against my cheeks. I declined dessert, and they offered me a ride back to campus.

My face reflected back at me in the back-seat window with every streetlight passed. The blue box with the capital H bolstered to the brown-bricked building glowed in the distant dark, breaking the reflection, and I was reminded of what I missed…whom I missed.

**12**
—

That night, I didn't notice if Deirdre was asleep in her bed. I didn't even wash my face or change out of my clothes into pjs. I just flopped belly-down onto my bed and allowed sleep to drag me under.

This made more work for me in the morning: I brushed my teeth twice, I washed my face only to reapply more makeup, I changed into another pair of clothes, added layers for the brittle conditions, and then I was out the door for work, my bag bouncing against my back.

On Tuesdays, I worked an open shift and had Contemporary Literature from 1 to 4 p.m., meaning I'd have plenty of time to stop by the hospital.

Marchie, again, was already counting the till, and again, after tying my apron, I completed the task for her. She looked at me over the top of her spectacles while arranging the pastry display.

"You know, that's bad for your eyes," I always told her. She'd always disapprove with a loud, "Hmph." She heard me—she just didn't want to listen.

"Drink of the day is London Fog." The short tone was her passive-aggressive way of telling me to keep my nose out of her business.

I grabbed the marker and walked around the counter to scrawl on the sign.

"You look tired," said Marchie. People seem to be braver with their words when they don't have to look a person in the eye. "A sad sort of tired," she continued. "Everything okay?"

"Just some things with my parents," I said. I flicked on the open sign and hoped a customer would open the door to interrupt the conversation.

"You want to talk about it?" she asked.

"I'm okay, Marchie."

She wiped around the buttons of the register and said, "I was your age once. I know how parents can be. But now that I am one, just know they don't do anything short of love." She had a son.

"How is Caleb doing?" I asked. "Is he enjoying a year off to work?"

A scowl was thrown my way as she said, "I think he likes it too much. I fear he'll never go back to school."

In walked the first customer and we placed a bookmark in the series of our life stories. The woman ordered a medium coffee and tipped us two dollars. After she left, a steady stream of students flooded the floor with their slush feet. One after the other, and with only Marchie and I on staff, it took longer to serve everyone than preferred. Many people seemed to be quite fond of London Fog.

One of the groups decided to situate themselves at one of the corner tables. Two of them tugged hulking books out of their bags, and I guessed that they were either math or science students. Another group flocked to a window seat. They looked like hipsters, but I didn't judge, I just admired—people-watching: faded denim, beanies, jagged haircuts. I often wondered what it would feel like for a person to dye their hair a shade of red and not care what others would make of it. Unfortunately, I lived my whole life caring about what people made of me.

The flood slowed to a trickle, and Marchie and I restocked the product, including several muffins in the pastry bane. We cleaned out the machines, wiped off the counters, and restocked the coin in the till.

The students' laughter often flew over the counter and forced me to lift my chin in observation, wondering what topics were being thrown about in conversation, wondering why the boy decided to get blonde streaks in his hair or why the girl was sporting plum lipstick.

"Do you know any of them?" Marchie asked, washing dishes in the backroom.

"No," I said, walking towards her. I put the cloth back in the sanitizer bucket.

"Then why are you staring?" she asked again. I shrugged my shoulders. All of a sudden, I heard chairs screech across the floor. When I turned the corner, I found that someone had spilled their drink.

I hollered, "Be right there!" to the hipsters.

I shuffled to the sink to grab the mop and bucket and caught the boy staring at me as I made my way back to their table.

"I'm sorry," said the boy with blonde streaks. "I'm an absolute klutz. I need to be more careful."

"It's okay," I said, twisting the mop then placing it in the department to squeeze the moisture out of the tassels. "It happens more times than you'd believe."

The drink landed next to the table so I didn't have to ask anyone to move their chairs. The blonde-streaked boy picked up the empty paper cup and tossed it in the garbage next to the door. Back and forth, back and forth, the mop made a sort of *swish* sound. They continued with their chatter, and I kept my head down until the stickiness disappeared, but then I heard, "...Harper." My nose twitched as if I could smell what they were talking about.

The girl with the plum lips talked. "I don't know, he just hasn't shown up to class this week."

"Yeah, but the teachers know. Mr. Rowling said it was some type of personal emergency," said the blonde-streaked boy.

"It's just unlike him is all," replied the girl with plum lips.

When I looked up to put the mop back in the bucket, I caught a glimpse of opened sketch pads and charcoal pencils spattered across the table. Harper is a visual artist?

I began wandering away with my thoughts when the boy with the blonde streaks called for my attention.

"Sorry, again," he said.

I continued walking to the backroom, lost in thought. I emptied the dirty water into the back lot and closed the door behind me.

"Not too much damage?" asked Marchie.

"Just some spilt coffee," I replied. The front door dinged, and I hustled to the register for a boy to order a pumpkin latte. I got his order ready, cashed him out and proceeded to the backroom to put the dishes away. Time moved swiftly and my shift change came quicker than planned. Gemma came in, said, "Hello," and told me, "Don't worry about balancing the till, I'll get to doing it. You just get to class."

"Thank you," I said.

After hanging my apron back on its peg, Marchie wished me a good day, and I told her I'd try.

Because the best any of us can do is try.

**13**

——

And that is what I did: try.

I tried my best to maintain focus in class. Today, we were studying modern contemporary writers from pop culture, which intrigued me, but even so, distracting thoughts kept tickling the back of my brain. But I didn't want to laugh and squirm at their perseverance; I just wanted to pay attention to Ms. Malaine's slide show.

I typed out notes. I didn't miss a beat, and I wrote every bullet point that Ms. Malaine motioned for us to remember.

"Contemporary literature began after World War II, its roots continuing to today. What makes contemporary literature different from other genres, such as fantasy and mystery, is that it deals with societal viewpoints. These viewpoints are then shown to the reader through a realistic character. Connections are then made to current events and social issues."

After she finished her lecture, she dismissed class a half-hour early after instructing us to: "Research a list of contemporary works of fiction and then point out the societal issue in each." I was about to leave the classroom when Ms. Malaine beckoned me over with a waving hand—I thought I was in trouble.

"Hi, Lora."

"Hi," I replied. My palms were coated in sweat, and I had to wipe them on my jeans.

"I just wanted to tell you that I've been rather impressed with the last couple of papers you've submitted," she said, leaning against her desk. "Writing comes naturally to you, or I get that feeling when reading your works. How's workshop class going?"

"Oh, it's going," I said. "Some days it's harder to write than others."

She nodded. "Of course, if you ever need a fresh set of eyes to look over your current novel, I'd be more than happy to."

"Thank you, Ms. Malaine," I said.

"No problem. Have a good rest of your day Lora."

It was the complete opposite of being in trouble, I thought to myself as I exited the building to walk to the bus stop. I checked the transit schedule nailed to a light post—the bus wouldn't come for another ten minutes. I took my headphones and Mp3 out of the side pocket of my bag and plugged the buds into my chilled ears underneath my hat (left then right). I had burned some CDs and downloaded the music onto the device for moments of waiting. City transit could fail people sometimes. Elton John was the first artist I came to love, and I blamed my mom for it. When she'd take me on errands, she told me that's the only thing she'd play in the van because it was the only soundtrack that would soothe me to sleep as I was buckled in a car seat. "Tiny Dancer" started playing as the bus rolled up. Thirty minutes and about eight songs later, the hospital loomed in my vision, and the bus came to the stop I needed.

Listening to music didn't give me time or space to worry. The lyrics took up the space and pushed away all other thoughts in my mind, but now I was anxious, standing on the cement sidewalk, the

44

hospital only a few strides away. Not knowing what to expect had always been one of the scariest things for me. Is Harper awake, or is he still fast asleep, protected from the dark events of his reality? I wished there was a way to protect people from themselves, but only the person who needs protecting can do that.

One foot in front of the other—that was what my mom told me to do in times of indecision. So, one foot in front of the other I went until I reached the familiar lobby, until I reached the familiar elevator.

Up button. Level four. Psychology.

Maggie's warm presence wrapped me up the moment the metal doors parted.

"For a moment I thought you weren't coming back," she said standing behind the nurse's station.

I shook my head. "I could never do that," I said. "Things just got busy yesterday."

"No worries," she said. "I'm just teasing. I told you to come only if your schedule allows. Go on," she said motioning toward the end of the hallway.

And again, one foot in front of the other, I walked down the familiar hallway with the familiar, buzzing lights and turned into the familiar room. But when I walked in, all familiarity was erased.

Harper was awake.

**14**

———

I blinked, and I'm thrown back ten years in time when some of the only things I had to worry about were if there were enough Oreos in the kitchen cabinet for tea parties and if I had a red crayon left in the box of my craft supplies. I never worried about finding the perfect tree to climb, but William did, and that was how he broke his arm, falling from a high branch of a tree in our backyard. I was eight years old. I remember crying as my Dad called 911. I remember I still cried, even as the ambulance backed into our driveway, even when Mom hugged her arms around me. I remember crying even still when Dad hopped into the back of the vehicle with William and Mom and I followed in her silver minivan.

"It's going to be okay, Lora. William just hurt himself," she said to me in the backseat. "The doctors will take good care of him, fix him up."

I still cried.

I didn't stop crying until I walked through the hospital doors and strutted towards the bed they were keeping him in, my clunky velcro shoes slowing me down. I touched the rough skin of his cast and one of the nurses walked up to me and asked, "Would you like to sign it?" She handed me a blue Sharpie. In big, scraggly letters I wrote L-O-R-A. It was only when I completed the last stroke of the A in my name that the tears had dried on my face and I felt okay again.

I faded back into the present, and William dissolved, replaced with brown hair and brown eyes—a stranger. Pinpricks of ice shot up my spine, climbing the bony rungs, and the frigid feeling climbed down my legs as well. I was immobile, stuck in the doorway. A burst of wind flew past my left ear, and I realized someone else had entered the room. It was Dr. Preston.

"Hi, Lora," he said, nodding his head, but he wasn't interested in my presence. He was studying the monitors and the chart clasped in his hand.

"Any headaches?" asked Dr. Preston. He waited patiently for any answer as Harper seemed hesitant.

"Somewhat."

"On a scale of one to ten how bad is the pain?"

"Seven."

"Good, one point down from last night."

*So, he woke up last night,* I thought to myself.

"Have you napped today at all?"

"No," he said.

"Did you eat breakfast and lunch?" Dr. Preston was thorough.

"Yes," he replied.

Dr. Preston wrote down some notes in the chart—a quick jot. "Good. Harper, I'll have a nurse bring you food in an hour or so. If anything changes, hit the call button," he said, motioning to the plastic piece with a red circle attached to a chord sitting on Harper's bedside table.

"Okay."

"And this," said Dr. Preston, taking his eyes off the file, "is Lora. She's the one who found you. Expect her company for a few days, but if having company bothers you, I can ask her to leave."

Harper swallowed what seemed to be a ball in his throat as his Adam's apple bobbed up and down then rested back in its place.

"It's fine," he barely whispered.

"Alright," said Dr. Preston. "I'll be checking in again late this evening."

He walked out the door, chart in hand, and left us alone in the room, its walls beginning to shrink around me. The window was too close, the monitors were too close, and Harper... Harper was much too close.

"You can sit, if you'd like," he said, pointing to the too-stiff chair positioned beside his bed, the same one I sat in a few days ago, the same one I sat in while he was still asleep. But now that he was awake, the chair seemed off, like I was looking at it through a fisheye. The colour and shape warbled. The warm brown seemed cooler and the stiff edges looked rounder. I settled in the chair, setting my backpack beside me on the ground. I kept my coat on, forgetting to take it off.

"How do you feel?" I asked, even though Dr. Preston covered the topic.

Harper cleared his throat. "You know that feeling you get when you've slept more than eight hours and you check the clock only to find out half the day is gone?"

I nodded in understanding. "I know it all too well." I offered a gentle smile, lips pressed together, only to break apart with my next sentence, "You feel like you're walking in fog all day until you finally get back to sleep."

"Exactly…" he said. His voice tapered off and his brows scrunched together. "Lora, I would like to apologize."

He threw the ball from left field, but I caught it anyway—sharp reflexes, or maybe I was just dedicated to observation. "Oh?" is all I could manage.

"I'm sorry. I'm sorry because the day you found me will probably be one of your least favourite days in your list of *My Least Favourite Days*. And, you don't seem like a girl who should have least favourite days, only favourites."

I smiled at his kindness.

I didn't know it then, but it wasn't *that* day that would be my least favourite, but another day entirely, that still revolved around him.

**15**

——

As an introvert, small talk wasn't my cup of tea, especially when meeting someone I didn't know. Words struggled against the closure of my throat, a narrow tunnel, and the vowels that wanted to form bounced off the walls of my teeth, but I tried my hardest for Harper. Talking to him while he was in a coma was much easier.

I explained the night I found him, but only because he asked three times after I said no. After the fourth time I gave in, even though I said, "I don't think it's good for the healing process," and he said, "Probably not, but I'd like to hear it anyway," and then I said, "Don't make me regret this." I didn't want him to tell Dr. Preston that I was torturing him, adding harmful memories to his mind.

But I told him anyway. I told him how I was walking home from work. He interrupted and asked, "Where do you work?"

I replied, "A campus cafe."

Then he asked where I went to school and I said, "University of Toronto."

"Me too," he replied.

"Alright, back to the story," I said. I got a few words in; it was chilly, I slipped on ice, and when I looked up…

"There you were."

He veered off the topic. "What are you taking?"

"I'm majoring in English and minoring in Creative Writing," I said, "What about you? You said you go to U of T too."

"Majoring in Visual Arts and minoring in History." I already predicted what his answer would be, apart from his minor. "Though, I haven't been to class in a couple days…obviously."

I nodded and started picking at a frayed string sprouting from the seam of my coat. He seemed to build a wall around what happened and pretended it wasn't there—out of sight, out of mind. He asked me all the unrelated questions he could.

"Hopefully, I can get back to maintaining attendance soon," he continued.

*So he cares about school*, I thought.

"What made you want to take English?" he asked.

"Um." No one had ever asked me this question before. "I suppose it sprouts from reading. I've been reading since I was little and, naturally, I fell in love with writing. The main white flag was English being my best class in high school."

"What book do you have on you right now?" he asked. My face bunched into confused lines.

"Come on," he said. "You're a reader. You must have a book on you at all times."

He wasn't wrong. I bent down and unzipped the second pouch of my backpack. I separated my current read from the rest of my school books so it wouldn't get damaged. My fingers found the soft cover, and I pulled out a copy of *Pride and Prejudice* by Jane Austen. He ripped the book from my hands and sat it on his lap, poking his finger into the back of his throat, gagging.

"Don't mock Jane Austen," I said. "It's a reread, and besides, I'm studying it in one of my classes."

He was flipping through the yellowed pages then stopped to stare at me. "You poor thing."

"Give me that," I said, taking back the book. I tucked it back into the second pouched and zipped the novel into safety, away from jesting.

"I'm just teasing," he said. "I can appreciate that you like classic literature. Not too many people do."

I started picking at the string again until the silky threads unraveled into a tuft of fuzz. "How about you?" I asked.

"I didn't always colour in the lines," he said. This made me laugh, the beats vibrating my chest. "But I was definitely infatuated with colours since I was a child. I found it fun and easy in high school, I got good grades too, so I thought, *Why not do it in university?* Might as well do something I'm good at."

He stared at the white sheet covering his legs and torso, biting his bottom lip, tearing away a layer of skin. "It also helps with things up here, you know," he said, tapping his right index finger against his temple. "When all the monsters roam free on a canvas, they don't seem so scary anymore."

I swallowed past the lump in my throat that formed with his words, and I blinked away the heat that started burning my eyes. "So," I began, "what's your favourite style, or method, or whatever you call it?"

"I prefer paint," he responded. "Not so much watercolours. I like the harsh acrylics. But, when I feel like it, I also enjoy sketching."

I couldn't ask any more questions because Maggie walked in carrying a plastic tray, Harper's dinner.

"It's that time already?" asked Harper.

"It is." Maggie smiled. She swung out the lap table and placed the tray on the fake wood. She took off the lid and exposed leathered roast beef, drowning mashed potatoes and fluorescent Jell-O. "I'll leave you two to it," said Maggie.

"Actually," I said, standing up, still dressed in my winter coat. "I should get going and let you eat—let you rest."

Harper nodded but looked surprised that he'd no longer have company, someone to talk to. Maggie already left the room, giving us privacy, and I shrugged my backpack onto my shoulders.

I turned to leave, but Harper's fingers clasped mine. I'd never held someone's hand before, aside from Mom and Dad. He had such a grip that I was forced to turn around, his brown eyes pinned me into place.

"Lora, promise me you'll come back."

He wedged his fingers even harder in between mine. "Come back tomorrow… visit me. Visit every day you can."

"I'll try, I'll always try," I told him. I looked down and both sets of our knuckles were turning white from his strength. I looked up and a tear had escaped from the cage of his bottom eyelid. He didn't relax until I said:

"I won't leave you, Harper."

**16**

———

One of the hardest things for humans to do is trust, especially someone who is unfamiliar. It is human nature to remain skeptical until finding reason not to be. If I were Harper, I would have been wiggling in bed all night. I wouldn't be able to sleep, thinking about the possibility that my only companion may never return—frightened from past events, frightened from meeting the person they saved, only to be more disappointed and more scared.

But I never left.

Not even when I made it back to the dorm that evening, walking into a scene of a placid Deirdre sitting on her bed, headphones in, watching *Friends*. I couldn't read her in the glow of the screen, but when she realized I was in the room, she took out her headphones, stopped the episode, and ejected the DVD from the disc drive in her laptop. I studied the floor while I felt her eyes study my face because I couldn't bear the weight of her stare.

She spoke first. "I'm sorry," she said. "I was harsh the other day, and I want to apologize. How you see things isn't wrong. I just care about you; I want you to be careful."

When I met her gaze, it wasn't as heavy as I expected. "I'm sorry, too. I didn't have to be so defensive."

She unfolded her limbs and stood up only to throw her arms around my neck, whispering again, in my ear, "I'm sorry." She pulled away and grabbed a coat from the bench at the end of her bed. "Have you had dinner yet?"

I shook my head. "Good," she continued, "I'm starving."

**17**

———

Even though we had turned in early, I still needed two shots of espresso in my coffee the next morning. This happened more often than not. I was grateful for only having one class on Wednesdays, but I wasn't so grateful that it was Novel Study—there was no room for grogginess when it came to Mr. Peterson. Each student had to sit, backs straight, notes open, to answer Mr. Peterson's questions about last week's readings.

He didn't call on me once, and I was able to sip on my coffee throughout the question and answer period. By the time he assigned the next readings for *Pride & Prejudice* and dismissed class, caffeine jitters were shaking my limbs, and I worried about being able to stand for my work shift.

Malcolm was sweeping the lobby and Gemma was restocking the pastry display when I walked in.

"Hey, Lora," called Gemma, her voice mixing with the customers'.

"Hey," I replied. "Has it been busy today?"

"Nothing too terrible," Gemma said while I hung my coat on the rack and tied my apron around my neck. "Marchie was able to go home early. I told her we could handle it."

I made my way to the till and started counting the coins, the copper and nickel clinking together, when a group of students walked through the door—the art students from the other day.

The boy with blonde streaks approached the till first and asked for a, "Matcha latte, please."

The girl ordered next. "A large mocha, please." And then the third wheel, a boy with thick, black-rimmed glasses and gelled hair:

"I'll take an earl grey tea."

"Is this together or separate?" I asked.

"Together," said the boy with blonde streaks.

"Ten dollars and seventy cents," I said.

The girl fished inside her tiny purse that dangled from her shoulder on a long chain and handed over the money.

"It'll just be a few minutes," I said. I turned around to help Gemma with the order.

"Enjoy," I said, placing the finished order on the counter.

I buried myself in the back sink for the next hour to get through the dishes and allowed Malcolm and Gemma to deal with orders.

I was transferring the pile of dishes from the rinse sink to the sanitizer sink when an uproar of voices penetrated the calm alcove I'd created for myself.

"Lora," called Malcolm. He peeked his head into the backroom and crept back a few steps from the tense scowl that my face was twisted into, like a dirty dish rag. "Spill at table two," he said hesitantly. That's the table next to the window. "Is it okay if you...?"

"Yeah, yeah," I cut him off. "Just have to get the mop ready, and I'll be right there."

I approached the table with the mop and bucket.

"I'm so sorry," he said. "I really need to watch where I throw my hands when I'm talking. At least we didn't have our sketches out yet."

The girl rolled her eyes. "That would have cost us an entire class."

"Again," he repeated, "I'm incredibly sorry."

He sat back down in his chair as I twisted the tangled mop into the bucket. It whined against the laminate as I pushed it back and forth.

"I hear he should be back by the end of next week," said the girl.

"It's about time," said the boy with thick-rimmed glasses. "I've missed Harper."

So these were Harper's friends. Now, I was certain.

"I'm still wondering what's made him miss a week," said the blonde-streaked boy.

So they don't know. Harper left his darkness where his friends wouldn't see it.

"I'm sure he'll explain everything," said the girl.

"I don't know, Abbie," said the blonde-streaked boy. "I don't know."

The mop stopped whining, and the art students stopped talking. I plunged the mop back inside its home and rolled it to the backroom where I opened the back door and poured the dirty water into the back-parking lot sewer.

After I washed my hands, I was met with Malcolm's trembling body. He was laughing.

Malcolm took over dish duty for me, and I helped Gemma with stocking product and orders. Soon, eight o'clock rolled around. I was done for the night.

**18**
———

During the bus ride, I hoped I wasn't too late. I hoped Harper would still be awake, but more so, I hoped he didn't think that I left him alone, that I gave up on visiting him, because I didn't.

I never did.

The blue H couldn't come fast enough. I stood up as soon as the bus neared the stop. I jerked forward and grabbed onto a rubber loop to steady myself.

"Thank you," I said to the bus driver, as I ran out the door.

My backpack crashed against my spine, only stopping once I stood still, waiting for the elevator. I was heaving and had to rest my hands on top of my knees.

The elevator dinged and split open for my eager body and fervent steps. I stood still for another moment, to catch my breath and slow my racing heart. I looked down and realized I was standing in a puddle from the melting snow that once clung to my boots. Two more deep breaths entered my body, and they reached far enough to steady the shaking.

I turned right into the very last room at the end of the hall. His room—Harper's room. The only source of light was a lamp that stood in the left corner near the window. The white, cotton sheet was pulled up to his neck, and his eyelids were fluttering in dream.

I crept my way to the chair beside his bed. It took me several seconds longer to place my bag on the floor and situate myself in the chair, but I didn't make a sound, and Harper remained asleep.

I was grateful that Harper was turned towards the window so I didn't have to stare at his face. I looked at his back, watching how his muscles shrunk and expanded with each drowsy breath, and I allowed these movements to soothe me.

I only stayed a minute longer—long enough to fish a sticky-note pad out of my backpack and to find a pen, writing:

Harper,

I stopped by after my work shift to see you, but you were asleep. Just wanted to let you know that I came and stayed a few minutes regardless. Hope you feel well tomorrow.

- Lora

I stuck the yellow square to his bed-side table and smeared my thumb over the sticky strip three times to make sure it would stay in place.

Until I rested my head on my pillow that night and fell asleep, I worried about the possibility of the yellow piece of paper lifting off the bedside table and falling to the floor. It would have seemed like I hadn't been there.

**19**

———

I had closed my locker and was surprised to see William's enthusiastic smile, making me squint through the cloudy day I was having.

"What do you want?" I had asked. I gripped my textbooks and pressed them as close as possible to my abdomen. "I need to get to class."

He walked with me the entire way, shoulder to shoulder, one glob of sticky tack keeping our shoulders together.

"Seriously, William." I stopped mid-stride, infuriated. My skin was growing in warmth, and I was sure to any passerby I was transforming into a red traffic light, but I didn't want anyone to stop and stare; I wanted them to go.

"I know you're having a bad day, so I just wanted to check on you," he said.

"I don't need you to check on me," I had spat. "It's not the end of the world." A sigh escaped my body, leading me to the closest set of lockers. I leaned against the metal hoping no one needed to get into one of them.

William walked closer to me. "You say that, but I know writing is your whole world."

Even though William was a year younger than me, he always spoke with the wisdom of a young adult. I shrugged, trying to get him off my back, even though it had been racking my conscience since first period. I had entered a national writing contest, and I didn't win. My creative writing teacher pushed me to enter, even though I didn't want to. I should have stuck to my guns and kept telling him, "I don't want to," but he told me, "You have what it takes, expose yourself, get out there."

I exposed myself. And got hurt.

"One contest doesn't define you," said William. "And I know it sucks right now because it's fresh, but by the time you enter the next one, you'll have forgotten about this."

I stared at the beam of light that cut across the tiled floor beside his foot, unable to make eye contact because I knew if I did, I'd end up a sobbing mess, and he'd have to hug me until his shirt became an overused human Kleenex. I didn't want hugs. I just wanted to get over myself but getting over yourself can be incredibly hard when emotion takes reign from logic.

"I have to get to class," I repeated. I peeled my back off the metal doors in a huff and left him alone in the hallway.

I remember I couldn't concentrate during history, and there were several times where I contemplated getting up to hide in the bathroom until the day was over. A movie was playing, but I didn't really see the characters or hear their words. I just saw clusters of pixels and made out bouts of gibberish.

I remember making the decision: I was going to give up writing, and I was 100 per cent certain about doing so, that is, until class ended, and I walked back to my locker. I spun the knob with its numbered sequence: 31 33 11. *Click*. The fish hook popped free and I hung it in its metal hole. After placing my books on the upper shelf I looked at the plain, grey wall of my locker door, only to realize that it wasn't so plain and it wasn't only grey—a yellow sticky note was stuck to the centre of the rectangle, its edges lifting up as if to poke me in the nose. In capital letters it said: I believe in you.

From the too-long sticks of letters and the exaggerated curves, I knew it was William who had left the reminder.

Without him, I would have given up.

But his sticky note had kept me going. I only hoped mine would keep Harper going too.

**20**

———

Today I was able to study at a nearby Starbucks and then catch a bus to the hospital where I'd spend my afternoon.

I walked through the doors five minutes after opening hour and the barista looked as though she wanted to push me right back out the door.

"What do you want?" she barked. Clamour rolled out of the backroom in the form of a floating stack of venti cups. I didn't realize someone was holding the cups until she placed them on the counter—the girl from the cafe I worked at.

"Sandy, that is no way to talk to customers," Abbie (I think her name was) said. She pointed to the stack of cups she left on the counter. "You can deal with those."

"What can I get for you?" she asked.

"Just a venti coffee with extra room for cream," I said. She told me the amount, and I fumbled with my wallet in my mitten hands then handed over the money.

"Keep the change," I said.

"Thank you."

I stood at the side counter while she made my drink and stared at the floor. At the café, I always felt rushed when the customer would stare at me making their beverage. It made me nervous. A tingling sensation spread through my face. Someone was staring at me.

"Hey, aren't you that girl from the coffee shop on campus?" Abbie asked, looking up while grinding the beans.

"Um, yeah," I replied, crisscrossing my ankles.

"I'm really sorry about Mika. He can be a pain." She looked back down to check the grind consistency.

"No worries," I said. I assumed she was talking about the blonde-streaked boy.

She placed the white cup underneath the coffee machine and lifted the lever, a stream of dark liquid poured out. "So, do you go to U of T too?" she asked over her shoulder.

"Yes," I said.

"Cool. What are you taking?" She wiped up a spill and the white cloth turned brown.

"English and Creative Writing."

"Right on, I can relate," she said. "I take Visual Art, though you may have figured that out already."

She placed the coffee on top of the counter and the black letters of my name were staring me in the face. "Here you go. Have a good day, Lora."

"You too," I replied.

I chose a spot as far away from the till as possible, a cozy corner with bar-stool seating. I placed my backpack in the seat beside me to discourage the closeness of strangers and settled my laptop on the wooden table. I turned the machine on and opened up my current project. Between the scurries of my fingers and the biting of my lips, I took sips of coffee to keep the words flowing. Type, bite, sip. Repeat.

I turned around and the coffee shop was now filled with people, almost every seat taken with dozens of filled coffee cups, and yet, I never heard a thing. Sandy was gone, and Abbie was too. I was ignorant to the shift change and new employees were behind the counter.

I pressed the save button on the top left corner of my screen and shut the laptop down, stowing it back into its pocket inside my bag. I put on my coat and headed out into the cold, walking to the bus stop.

When I reached the hospital lobby, I embraced the heat and scraped my boots against the rubber matt. When I got to level four, Maggie wrapped me in a hug.

"How are you?" she asked. "How are classes?"

"Good, actually. I would have gotten here earlier, but I was working on a project," I said, lifting the left strap of my backpack between my fingers.

A voice from behind startled me. "She's a reader. Didn't you know that Maggie?" Harper was standing proud in a hospital gown, wiggling his eyebrows. "I bet you're a writer too. Creative writing and all."

I glanced at Maggie and she struggled to hide a smirk. "Get back in your room," she said. "Walking time is over."

"You have to make sure these limbs still work," he said clapping both of his thighs. "I lay in bed so long my muscles just might forget how to function."

"Very funny. Room. Now," she demanded. "Lora can help you find your way if your muscles forget somewhere between here and your room."

Harper spun around and threw a friendly wave over his shoulder for Maggie to catch. I glanced at her and her returning smile. Harper started walking already so I followed him.

He waited until I caught up with him, walking shoulder-to-shoulder to tell me, "I got your sticky note, by the way."

"Okay," I said.

"It was sweet," he said. I felt his eyes inspecting my face for some sort of reaction, but he couldn't see underneath my skin, so the bubbles of nerves that were beginning to burst were safe from recognition.

"I just didn't want you to think I didn't come... or forgot about you," I replied.

We entered his room and he crawled into bed, propping up the three pillows behind his back. He left the sheet at the foot of the bed. I took my seat in the usual stiff chair and deposited my backpack in its usual spot on the ground, leaning against the leg of the usual stiff chair.

"It means more than you know."

I looked up then, which was a mistake, because his dark brown eyes found my blue ones, and they latched on. I didn't think he'd ever let go. I didn't think my heart would ever stop banging against the walls in my chest. But eventually ,he did let go.

"You haven't removed it." I pointed to the sticky note.

"I didn't feel the need to. I kind of like looking at it, a reminder." He cleared his throat.

"So, Dr. Preston told me I should be out of here by this time next week, but," he said, leaning over towards the other bed-side table, "only if I attend one of these."

He sprawled five pamphlets in an arc on his lap. They all had the word "therapy" printed at least once on the cover. I swallowed past a knot that rolled itself from my chest up into my throat. I thought about William and how he should have had these opportunities. Harper tucked in his bottom lip to meet his top, applying pressure and whitening his skin.

"It's not all bad," I said, or so I liked to hope. His face was pure worry.

"Look," I said leaning over, picking up one with warmer tones. "This one doesn't look so bad."

He took the paper from my hand and read the cover. He then opened it up, flipped through a few pages and threw it back onto his lap in frustration.

"This is pointless, I'm not ever going to get any better. I've been dealing with this since I was 16."

I assumed "this" meant depression, but I had to ask. "This?"

"It's an ongoing cycle of sadness, and I can't crawl out of it. I can tell myself I have friends who care, I can tell myself I have things going for me with school, I can tell myself these things one hundred times a day, but the sadness still stays, and I still feel worthless."

I wondered if William ever felt the same way, and I wondered why he never told anybody. I wished he would have.

This is the first time I had seen Harper outside of the covers and my eyes fixed on his hands, rearranging the papers, which made my gaze float to his wrists where white bandages were still wound. I worried that if I stared too long and too hard that he might get uncomfortable.

He picked up the pamphlet I originally chose and placed it on top of the yellow sticky note. "I'll tell Dr. Preston I'm interested in this one, I guess." He took the other four and put them back onto the other bedside table. He slouched against the stack of pillows, as if in defeat. "It makes me feel stupid," he said.

"What does?"

"This."

He pointed to the pamphlets. He pointed to the plastic rail attached to the bed. He grabbed the thin fabric of his hospital gown, pinching it between his thumb and pointer finger, and he circled the white bandages with his own fingers.

"You aren't stupid, Harper," I said. "There's nothing stupid about this situation, or who you are, or what you feel."

This time when his eyes met mine, I held on, trying to offer as much sympathy possible.

**21**

———

Harper looked like he could either cry or hug me, and I'd never done well with either from anyone, so I was thankful when Dr. Preston walked through the door for his checkup.

After going over his charts and monitors, he talked to Harper. "So, have you chosen one yet? You've had them since yesterday, and I need to arrange some things with the company before next week."

"This one," said Harper, taking the brown paper off the night table. I checked to make sure the sticky note wasn't stuck underneath. It was still pressed against the table.

Dr. Preston took the paper in his hand and gave it a once-over. He flipped it over to read the back and then flipped to the front once again. He clipped it to Harper's chart and walked out of the room.

"He scares me sometimes," said Harper.

A laugh escaped my lips and I quickly pressed them back together to hide my outburst.

"Yes," I said. "He can be rather intimidating."

Harper's eyebrows lifted, asking me a question. "Don't you have class?"

"Not until five."

"What about homework?" he asked.

"I already did some before coming here."

"And work?" he asked again.

"I don't work today."

"So, you're stuck with me all afternoon," he said, grinning.

"I guess you could say that, though, I wouldn't necessarily use the word 'stuck.'"

"Did you do some more writing today?" Harper asked.

I narrowed my eyes and pursed my lips. "Why are you so interested in what I do?"

"Because you're interesting," he said. "At least, to me you are. So, did you?"

"Yes."

"What are you working on? What genre?"

"It feels like a test with the number of questions you ask me," I said.

"Oh, I'm sorry. My friends often tell me that I talk too much around new people."

I tucked a piece of hair behind my ear. "This may seem weird," I said. "But I know your friends. Well, not actually *know* them; I've just seen them at work."

"Where do you work again?" he asked.

"The campus cafe."

His eyes widened, and I worried that they'd fall out of his skull—that I'd have to catch them. "We go there all the time, mainly for sketching. We can't bring full canvases around with us. It's also where we can just relax for a few hours, before or after classes."

"Yeah, um, your friend, the one with blonde streaks, is kind of a klutz, and I've had to clean up his mess twice, and I accidentally

72

overheard conversation, and your name popped up. I thought it was too much of a coincidence for them to not know you."

"That sounds like Mika," Harper said.

"And Abbie served me today at Starbucks," I said.

His gaze floated to the ceiling, to the line where the wall meets it, and my own gaze followed soon after to make sure there wasn't a bug or some strange image forming.

"You know, they miss you," I continued. He was still contemplating the spot on the ceiling.

"I know," he said.

"They don't know at all about...?"

"No," he cut. "And I'd rather it be kept that way."

"Harper, things like this are easier when you have a support system."

"They won't understand; nobody understands." He shifted his gaze to the ground.

*But I do understand*, I thought to myself—William.

"I can empathize more than you'd like to believe," I said.

His facial expression took on a mask of knowing, of hurt and sympathy. It was one of those faces only a small portion of the population can wear, one of the ones that say, "I know where you've been, and no one should ever have to go there in their lifetime."

"I've never had a support system, Lora," he said. "I find it easier to deal with things alone." I wanted him to try because William didn't.

"You can always try," I said.

He shook his head. "I can't. I'm too much for people, Lora. I'm too heavy. It's why I'm here."

"Those thoughts are only in *your* head, Harper, no one else's."

"Eventually, you'll get sick of me, knowing what you do about me. It's why I've never told my friends. Label me liability."

My eyes burned. It hurt to hear the words he said. It hurt to realize how warped the image was of himself that he saw. But it hurt the most to have him believe that I saw him that way too—I didn't.

"But you aren't, Harper, and you need to stop talking to yourself that way." He turned his face away from mine to stare out the window. "What if I went with you?" I asked.

He turned back to face me. "What?"

"What if I went to your sessions with you?" I repeated. "I don't think I'll be able to sit in the room with you, but I could hold-up in the waiting room. I could walk with you or drive the bus with you, too."

Speculation scrunched his features. "Why are you offering all this?"

"Like I said, I can relate to this more than you know."

## 22

Next week came with blinding speed.

Everything felt like a blur: Mom and Dad's visit over the weekend, my morning work shifts, my afternoon work shifts, my morning classes, my afternoon classes, and my all-day classes.

Eventually, and too soon, Thursday rolled around. No matter how hard I pressed my foot against the brake pedal, the week didn't slow down.

I didn't go to Starbucks and write like I usually did Thursday mornings. Instead, I went right to the hospital to meet Harper.

When I got there, I waited at the nurses' station with Maggie for about half an hour. She told me that, "Dr. Preston is just going over some paperwork with him that he has to sign."

She talked about her kid again and went on to ask me how school was going. I told her it was going "great." And she told me, "That's good to hear. You seem like a smart girl." I nodded my head and she continued. "So, Harper says you're a reader."

"Yes," I said.

"What's your favourite book?" she asked—one of the hardest questions to answer.

"Um…"

She rephrased the question: "Or, at least one of your favourites."

"Well, I've always appreciated *The Catcher in The Rye,* though I know many people don't like the writing and don't understand the meaning of the story."

"Oh yes. Is that the fellow who writes about war and banana fish?"

"Yes, he is that fellow. J.D. Salinger," I said laughing.

"What's a banana fish?"

Harper stood so close to me that if I wasn't talking to Maggie, I would have felt his breath on the back of my neck. My body vibrated in surprise, a quick pulse.

"Is it a fish that looks like a banana? I feel like that would be too easy," he said.

I almost didn't recognize Harper in regular clothing: blue Levi's, a Tommy Hilfiger sweater, and a Roots coat. He looked like a completely different person, a stranger almost.

Dr. Preston leaned against the desk, his elbow and forearm covering the surface. "Lora, I understand you offered to accompany Harper to therapy. Make sure he goes, okay?"

"I will," I said.

Harper started walking towards the elevators, and I tried to catch up when Dr. Preston tapped my shoulder. "If he doesn't go, please contact me." He handed me a white business card with black letters stating his name and phone number.

"Okay," I said.

*But there was no way he wasn't going to go*, I told myself.

I walked down the hallway until I was next to Harper. When the elevator dinged, we walked through the doors together.

Side by side.

**23**
———

"I forgot to ask," I said, the thrum of the elevator jiggling my voice, "Where do you live?"

"I stay on campus."

"Me, too," I said.

The elevator stopped moving and the doors opened, exposing the lobby. I stepped out first and Harper followed. I watched his apprehensive movements. He walked with his feet close together, a timid shuffle, and I thought a string was tied around both of his ankles, limiting his stride.

"I don't really know where to go from here," he said.

"Just follow me."

We exited through the ER doors, the first set of doors I entered—the first set of doors that lead me to Harper. As we took steps away from the lobby, away from the hospital and its doctors, worry began to squeeze my heart. I wouldn't be going back there anymore to visit Harper because he'd be here, near me, on campus. And I already missed it—the safety of the building that level four provided. Without the bed and the room, Harper's illness became all the more real and scary, because we walked away from a place that guaranteed his safety. On campus, in society, anything could happen. Doctors were no longer a call button away.

"You okay?" he asked. I forgot I had to keep walking.

When we reached the bus stop, I told him, "You won't have to remember where this stop is located because you won't be using it."

"It's okay, Lora, I know how transit works," he said.

"Right, sorry."

When we got on the bus Harper sat next to me, and I found it strange. I always rode the bus alone and tried to stay away from strangers. I'd move seats if there was an empty one with no one next to it. I didn't expect him to sit across from me or one seat over. I just wasn't used to an intentional presence. His coat brushed mine and I found myself scooting an inch the other way.

I was happy when the bus finally reached campus because it meant I could breathe again. I was holding my breath the whole ride, my body's reaction to someone who was too close.

We stepped off the bus, and I watched Harper's breaths float into the baby blue sky. He formed his own clouds. He stopped, closed his eyes, and tilted his face to the sun.

"What are you doing?" I asked. I had to stop walking. Maybe he had sensitive eyes.

"Just taking it in," he said.

"The campus?"

"Goodness, no. The sun. I missed it."

I shook my head and I could feel the pom-pom on my toque bob back and forth, placing its weight on my scalp.

"So which building are you? East or West?" I asked.

He opened his eyes and looked at me. "East," he said.

"I'm in the West building. We can go to yours first to get you situated."

"Okay," said Harper.

We walked in silence. It was odd to think that he'd been living on the same campus as me all semester, across the courtyard. Our paths may have even crossed walking around campus, the hallways of art buildings, ordering drinks at Starbucks—but I'd never known. You could glimpse a stranger's face for a split second and not remember their features, even if you see them again and again. Maybe I saw Harper but just didn't *look*.

"Are you going to be okay?" I asked.

He shoved his hands in his pockets, the bag of his belongings being squished between his side and elbow. "What do you mean?"

"I just—I mean, will you be okay? To continue living on campus? Is your roommate around often?"

"Lora, I don't need a babysitter," he said, a smile splitting his face in half. "I'll be okay, I am okay. Besides, my roommate is in my circle of friends."

My mind drifted to Ophelia, and I wondered what it would be like to have her as my roommate instead of Deirdre—someone who shares the same passion for English and writing.

"You lucked out with that," I said. "I'm assuming he's an art student too?"

"Why, of course," replied Harper. "Artists must stick together in a world that seems so left-brained."

He paused, squinting at the sun. He looked like he was in pain and I thought that maybe he had sensitive eyes. But it wasn't the sun that was causing him pain. "Though, I think it's my right brain that is my hamartia."

"Harper, please don't talk like that." His words crushed me; my chest burned and my feet grew heavier with each step.

"It's the right side of my brain where the thoughts manifest, but it's also where they can be released, though releasing them doesn't do anything. They just form pretty lines and splotches on a canvas for people to gawk at, but what they don't realize is that they're gawking at someone's pain. Hamartia."

His words stung, and I stopped walking.

The pavement melted to auditorium seats, and I was back in high school, watching William play Peter in *Peter Pan*. I was so proud of him when he told me on the bus home that he got the role, and I was even more proud when I saw him wear the forest-green tights, shirt and hat with a red tuft. When it came time to bow, I was the first to stand, my hands slapping frantically together, my fingers tingly from the severe pressure. When the actors and actresses left the stage, they were beacons, but it didn't matter because another source of pain took over—I smiled so much my face hurt. I just thought William had always liked theatre, but maybe it was where he expressed his pain too. If it was expression, if I knew this at the time, then I would have fallen to my knees and begged him to keep trying.

"Lora?"

*Just keep trying,* I would have told him.

"Lora?"

*I love you,* I would have said. And still do.

"Lora, are you okay?"

Someone's fingers clasped my left arm, and I was startled from my auditorium seat. I wriggled free, uncertain as to why he'd grabbed me.

"Are you okay?" Harper repeated.

"Yes, sorry," I said.

"Are you sure?" We continued to walk, and the East building was only a few steps away.

"I'm certain. I just get bad headaches sometimes. I forgot my sunglasses," I lied.

I didn't have sensitive eyes either.

**24**

———

Our conversation dwindled as Harper waved his pass to unlock the building's doors. I was about to ask what floor number his room was located but a flurry of blonde hair leaned over the staircase banister. I couldn't see who the person was because their face was hidden behind a curtain of bangs.

"Blasted, is that you, Harper?" He leaned even further over the banister and I was afraid that he was going to fall. I'm not strong enough to catch him. "I thought I heard your voice."

He leaned back from the edge of the stairs and bounded down to the lobby—the boy from the cafe, Mika.

"I didn't know when you were coming back," he said, wrapping one arm around Harper's shoulders. Harper looked uncomfortable but tolerated the gesture anyway. Mika pulled away, sensing the stiffness of his stance, or his apprehension.

"And who is this?" asked Mika.

I couldn't possibly tell Mika the truth and say, "Oh, I'm the girl who found your friend half-dead on a side street."

So instead I said, "His cousin," while Harper started saying, "She's…"

He turned to me, eyebrows raised and lips parted. I could tell he wanted to ask me what made me say this, why the cover, but I knew he understood when he pressed his lips back together; he didn't have a better explanation, or one that wouldn't sound crazy if he wanted to keep Mika on the outside.

"Yeah, she's my cousin," Harper confirmed.

"Cool," Mika exclaimed. "Didn't know you had a cousin. I'm Mika," he said, offering me his hand.

I shook it. "Lora."

"Nice to meet you Lora." His gaze shifted to Harper. "So why were you gone for a week?"

"Personal issues," replied Harper.

"You sound like the teachers," said Mika. Harper's ears grew red from lobe to tip, a chameleon transforming, only red isn't suitable camouflage for emotions. "Whatever, though, your business is your business."

Mika grabbed onto the railing and climbed the first flight of stairs. "Why are we taking the stairs?" asked Harper.

"I need more exercise," said Mika. "Or so my mom tells me."

"Did she visit this week?" Harper asked.

"Of course, and you know what she said? 'Mika, by the time you're graduated you won't be able to fit into any of your clothes. You need to eat better, darling.' Yet, I haven't gained a pound. I checked just to prove her wrong."

"She's just paranoid," said Harper.

I followed them and tried not to laugh at their banter. Mika turned his head over his shoulder to look at me. "When my parents got divorced, my dad packed on the pounds. That's why she's worried—that I'll become just like him."

I bit my lip, not knowing what to say. That must have been rough. We were on the second stairwell now and I could feel sweat starting to trickle down my back underneath my dense, winter coat.

"One more to go," said Mika. So Harper's room is on level three. I would have suggested the elevator if I knew this. Mika could get his exercise on his own time.

"So how old are you, Lora?" asked Mika.

"Twenty," I said.

"So two years younger than Harper. You guys must have been real close growing up."

"Like this," replied Harper. His middle finger was crossed over his pointer—fingers crossed Mika wouldn't call his bluff.

We reached the hallway of level three and turned left only to turn right after a few paces. Mika stopped outside room 303 and swiped his card in the slot. The door unlocked.

Even though their dorm had beds and a bathroom, it looked like an art studio: two easels next to the window, discarded canvases covering the floor, desks marked with paint and pastel, and there was a black, oblong line streaked across the bathroom door. I stepped into the room, leaning against the wall, pointing my finger.

"Don't ask," said Mika. "We were intoxicated and somehow Harper thought the door was a canvas."

"*I* thought the door was a canvas?" exclaimed Harper. "That was all you Mika."

"Right," Mika said, taking a seat at his desk. "Wouldn't want to make you look bad in front of your cousin."

I was about to ask, "What are you talking about?" when I remembered the lie I'd created. I had to remember to play along. Mika crossed his legs and sported an exaggerated grin.

"I was going to order some pizza. Would you like to stay and hang out, Lora?"

Harper's eyes were eager when they met mine. I pulled my phone out of my butt pocket, checked the time, and put it back into its place.

"I would love to," I said. "But, unfortunately, I have class in 45 minutes, and I should really get going, but thank you for the offer. It was nice meeting you, Mika."

I was about to leave the room, but Mika's words forced me to halt. "Aren't you going to say good-bye to your cousin?" he asked.

*Oh, right,* I thought to myself. *Play along.*

I walked over to Harper and his arms opened naturally, as if we'd hugged each other one hundred times before over Lego houses and rainy mud pies. But I didn't grow up with him, and this was our first hug. His arms tightened around my waist, and I thought my stomach was going to climb out my mouth, but I don't think that would have been possible because it would have been slammed down by the frantic beats of my heart. I only hoped Harper couldn't feel the persistent drum through my coat. He let go, and I'm pretty sure his face mirrored mine, a warm blush spreading to the parts of my skin concealed under my coat. I backed up.

"Come around any time," said Mika.

I glanced at Harper one last time before leaving the room and I didn't like what I saw. His eyes were ablaze, a dozen tiny sparklers dancing in each of his pupils.

I thought my ears were playing tricks on me as I heard the whine of a door behind me. I was already halfway to the stairs.

"Lora. Lora, wait up a second."

It was Harper.

It was Harper walking towards me.

He was blushing. I was blushing. We looked like a pair of flamingos. I stopped and turned to face him.

"I was wondering," he said sheepishly, "if I could get your number, so I can let you know when my therapy sessions are and such, if you still wanted to go, I mean."

His hands were clasped behind his back but when I said, "Oh, sure," he broke free revealing a pen and paper, offering both of the supplies. I took the pen and used the hallway wall as a table to write down the ten digits. I handed back the pen, capping it, and folded the paper.

"There you go," I said.

"Thank you," he replied. "See you later." He waved and turned back to his partly opened dorm door.

I shook my head as I walked to the stairs and down each staircase.

Three.

Two.

One.

*What are you doing to me, Harper Engels?*

**25**

———

"Deirdre?" I called out in the empty room. Part of my voice cocooned itself in the tangle of bedsheets while another part bounced off the bedroom walls.

"Deirdre?" I called again. She poked her head out of the bathroom.

"What's up?" She held a tube of eyeliner in her hand, her right eye significantly bolder than her left.

"I'm heading out now, I'll be back Sunday night." I double-checked the room to make sure I wasn't forgetting anything and made myself dizzy, spinning in a circle. Round and round, then back around again, hair whipping me in the face.

She capped the tube and twisted it closed. She walked over to me, her arms squeezing my neck too hard.

"I'll miss you," she said.

"It's just a weekend," I replied.

"But still, your lack of presence makes a difference. Who will I eat pizza and watch *Friends* with?" Her pout turned into a smile. "I hope you have a good time."

"I will. See you Sunday."

"See you," she said.

I hoisted my bag and walked out of the room, closing the door behind me, and made my way down the hall to the elevators. *No more staircases this week,* I told myself. As I was waiting for the elevator, I received a text from my mom saying she and Dad were waiting in the parking lot. I texted back:

**BE DOWN SOON.**

After hitting "send," the doors opened, and I stepped inside. The elevator shook to a stop as the doors opened to the lobby. I pushed open the front, glass door to the building and was engulfed in a sheet of white. It was snowing, which made me a bit worried for the commute home. My boots' soles were already lost in the frozen fluff.

Dad was waiting for me, leaning against the SUV. He popped the hatch and helped me place my things inside. Closing the hatch, he pulled me into a one-armed hug and said, "Missed you."

"Missed you, too," I said, though the exchange was hard to hear through my earmuffs.

I settled into the back seat and Mom didn't waste a minute to get on my case. I didn't even close the door. "So how has this week been?" she asked.

"Good," I said. "I work four to five days a week between classes."

"That's excellent, Lora," she said. Dad put the key and ignition and backed out of the lot and onto the city streets. "It's not too much though, right? You're still finding time for homework and assignments?"

"Yes, Mom," I said.

"How's Deirdre?" she asked. "We still need to have her over for dinner. From what you've told us, she seems like a sweet girl."

"She is," I said. "And I'm sure she'd like that."

"Are you okay if we head right home? I have a recipe cooking in the crock-pot. Do we need to stop anywhere for errands?"

"No, Mom, that sounds fine."

"I made a roast," she said, "your favourite."

"Thanks, Mom." We smiled at each other through the driver's mirror.

I unzipped my backpack I brought with me in the back seat and plucked out my Mp3—snowy weather and car rides made me sleep, and listening to Elton John would make me fall asleep even faster.

*And I guess that's why they call it the blues*
*Time on my hands could be time spent with you*
*Laughing like children, living like lovers*
*Rolling like thunder under the covers*
*And I guess that's why they call it the blues*

When I opened my eyes, we were parked in a driveway and auburn bricks burned through the blizzard.

I was home.

**26**

___

The bricks continued to burn my eyes, even after I grabbed my bags and walked into the foyer—everything was orange. It felt weird to be home again. It was like grasping for a familiar memory that was out of reach, unable to retrieve the tiny details that made the memory intimate, important. I dropped my bag, and my fingers hung limp in space, frozen in the air, unable to curl, unable to hold onto the details. This house (home) would no longer be my intimate place anyway, and all the memories wouldn't remain stuck to its walls and hidden in its carpets. New people would wash away the fingerprints and dirt, vacuum away the memories too, and make it their own memories to paint on the walls, to hide in the carpets— memories that would no longer be ours, or mine.

Mom started walking up the stairs, so I took my bag and followed her up the two flights. We turned down the hallway and walked to the dead end, turning right into my room. The door was already open, and the lamp on my bedside table made a feeble attempt to brighten the corners of my baby-blue room with its tungsten glow, the yellows and blues mixing into green. I felt sick. Even though the edges of my room were left in shadows there were illuminated cardboard boxes that dotted the floor. Three of my dresser drawers were open—emptied.

"I already started packing for you, I hope you don't mind," said Mom. "I just didn't want you to feel stressed on top of school and work. I want to make this as simple as possible for you."

There was nothing simple about the six brown walls of each box. There was nothing simple about my three empty dressers. It was difficult—all of it, and tears pierced my eyes. I didn't want to cry, but the heat built and built and my throat threatened to close completely. The inability to breathe wouldn't be nearly as painful as looking at all this emptiness.

"Lora, honey, are you okay?" Mom stared at me with brows furrowed. She never wore a frown well.

"Yes, fine. I just have to get used to it."

"Oh, honey," she said, pulling me into her side, pressing my head against her shoulder with her hand over my ear. Her voice was an echo. "I promise you, you'll love the new house. And your room is twice the size as this one, *and* you will have your own bathroom."

But size didn't matter. My room could be as small as a shoe box and I'd remain happy because it would be *my* room in *my* burning brick house.

She shifted her feet and stepped away. "I'm going to go check on the roast and set the table. Come down when you have your things put away, okay?"

"Okay," I said. But what was there to put away when there was so much I had to pack?

I dropped my backpack onto my desk chair that sat next to the window and abandoned my duffle bag at the end of my bed. I didn't bother unpacking. Usually, I'd fold my clothes into neat squares and lay them in my dresser, but not this time. The times of perfect squares are over. I felt out of place, a ship without an anchor, unable to properly settle into a room that will no longer be mine. Thoughts of moving exhausted me, and I flopped face-first onto my bed, hugging my pillow, squishing my face in the cotton. I wished I could hide here forever and wondered if the new family would adopt me as one of their own. If only just so I could stay here.

My hand touched something scratchy, and I pulled out a piece of folded paper. It looked like it was ripped out of a notebook, its frayed edge mimicking static meeting hair. I turned onto my back and unfolded it once, twice and three times. Even though the paper was charted into six rectangles from the folds it was easy to depict the blueprinting—a letter. The lines of the letters looked more like squiggles. I read the date. William would have been about seven years old.

*Dear sister,*

*You are the bestest sister in the entire world. No one is better than you, that's truer than true.*

*Love,*

*Will*

I hugged the paper to my chest, the corners folding against my collar bones. I laughed. It was so juvenile; the rhyming, the exaggeration, but at seven years old you wouldn't see it that way.

I wondered how William *would* see me if he was still here—if I'd still be the bestest sister in the entire world.

**27**
———

I never got used to the empty seat at the dining table. It always felt alien because it would forever remain untouched—an elephant in the room with the word *William* written on it in invisible marker. My cheeks grew hot, and it wasn't because of the steaming meal. Mom passed me the gravy. I took the stainless-steel handle between my fingers and drowned my beef and potatoes in the thick liquid. The quiet didn't help to cover the feeling that something was missing. I wondered how my parents fared without me being home.

"So, what are you currently working on in class?" Dad asked.

"Which class?" I replied.

"Well, are you working on a book, a project of some sort?"

"A book," I replied.

The screeching of silverware on ceramic plates made me wiggle in my seat and my shoulders meeting my ears. My elbows dropped back down to my waist and I tried to relax.

"Well that's exciting," said Mom. "How far along are you?"

"Almost halfway."

The buzz from my jean pocket startled me. I forgot I put my phone in my pants when walking inside the house. I scooped another mountain of potatoes and shoved them in my mouth. My phone buzzed again. I swallowed and grabbed another bite. And, it buzzed. *Again.* And then again.

Mom cleared her throat. "Lora, you know how I feel about devices at the table."

"Sorry, Mom," I said. "It's probably just Deirdre."

"Doesn't she know you're with your family this weekend?" Mom replied.

"Yes, she does, I told her before I left. She's probably just talking to me about something important."

"How important could it be to interrupt dinner?" she asked.

"Right, sorry," I said again. "I forgot I had put it in my pocket. I'll go put it in the kitchen."

My chair screeched as it slid against the hardwood floors and I couldn't help but flinch. Phone in hand, I padded into the kitchen and set the device on the countertop next to the frosted cake for dessert. Mom was a stress baker. If she felt anxious or sad, she'd open one of her cookbooks, and in the next hour or so she'd be offering a plate of muffins or cookies to whoever was in closest vicinity.

After sitting back down at the dining table, we focused on our food and conversation was lost to the bites of meat and swigs of water. When the plates were emptied, I helped Mom and Dad load the dishwasher and clean off the table.

"Oh, shoot, I forgot to pick up some butter. I wanted to make cookies."

"Dear," said Dad, "we don't need cookies, we already have a cake. And it looks delicious."

"But a cake isn't cookies," she said.

I walked into the kitchen. My parents stood at the sink, one washing dishes while the other one dried. "The cake is perfect, Mom."

"But I was going to make them for tomorrow, as a little treat for packing since we'll be at it all day." She twisted the drying towel in both hands, forming a stressed bridge between fists. "Lora, do you think you could walk to the corner store and grab some butter?"

"But it's freezing out and there's snow on the ground. Can you wait till the dishes are done, and then I can go pick some up?" asked Dad.

"I do suppose so," said Mom.

"I'll go with you," I said.

So, when the dishes were done, and when the plates and cups were set on the drying rack, I shoved my feet back into my boots. The walk would have been about eight minutes, but given the weather it would have felt longer, and probably would have taken longer to avoid slipping on black ice.

Black ice.

I remembered the last time I slipped on the deceiving surface and thought about where it had led me—maybe a deceiving scenario.

When Dad parked the car, I told him I'd go in, and that it would only be about five minutes.

"Hey, oh my gosh, Lora."

I was surprised to see a familiar face. Apparently, Seth's mom had the same idea—baking, except he held a carton of eggs.

"How've you been?" he asked.

Seeing Seth was like seeing William's twin, that is, if he had a twin. Seth and William had been inseparable. You never found one without the other. They were the image of best friendship. But these days, you only found the one. There was no other.

Spores of pain drilled holes into my heart, leaking out all the painful memories. I had hung out with them often, as we were close in age. Many movie and ice cream dates. But it all stopped...

I moved forward, opening my arms. "Seth, hi."

He returned the hug without cracking the eggs. "I'm doing well, what about you? How is high school going?"

"It's not too bad. I can't really complain." William would have been a senior this year, I thought to myself, staring at the stubble pricking Seth's chin. I bet William would have had to shave too.

"Do you have an idea as to what you want to get into yet?"

He shifted his weight from his left foot to his right—uncertainty. "Not really, but after Christmas break, I'll write down my options. My parents are getting antsy." William would have been prepping for college too. Or university, but he seemed like the college type—hands-on.

"Well, I have to get this butter back home," I said, lifting the bar in my hand.

"Man, I really do miss your mom's baking. It feels like I used to have it every day," said Seth.

Every day until William killed himself. Someone was stacking marbles at the back of my throat, and I couldn't balance the structure on the slope of my tongue. The balls started rolling around and they crashed against the sides of my throat. I coughed and a tear slid down my cheek. I covered my cough with my coat sleeve and wiped the tear with it as well. It looked like it was never there.

"Well, see you around, Lora. Tell your parents I say hi."

"Of course," I replied. "Feel free to stop by. Don't be a stranger."

But when strings are dropped because the hands that held them are gone, we all become strangers, an assortment of balloons floating in different directions. Some of us will bump into each other here or there... but some will never meet again. And some balloons float too high into the atmosphere and break upon pressure.

William: a balloon that popped.

**28**

———

"Something tells me you did more in there than purchase a brick of butter," said Dad.

"I bumped into Seth," I said.

"Seth," Dad repeated, probably sifting through his file of memories while backing onto the street. "You mean that kid who was over so much he felt like an adopted child?"

"That's him," I said.

"Jeez, it seems like forever since I've talked to him. And yet, he used to feel like one of my own."

Things change.

"You got the unsalted kind, right?" Dad asked.

"Yes," I replied.

"Good, we wouldn't want to upset your mom. She really wants to bake these cookies."

"So I've seen," I said. "Has she been okay?"

"Yes, she is just stressing more because of the move, but I know it'll be good for all of us."

I nodded, hoping he could see me in the dark car. The tires stopped on the driveway, and Dad and I tread footprints into parts of the untouched snow, cracks outlining the ovals made by our feet.

"I was beginning to worry," said Mom as soon as we entered the house. "I was about to call you, but I saw the both of you left your phones here."

"Sorry, dear," Dad said, planting a kiss on her cheek. "Lora saw Seth and she stopped to say hi."

"He was getting eggs," I said. This piece of information was irrelevant, but I wanted my casual words to dilute the awkwardness that started the steep the air.

"And how is he?" Mom's smile was pulled too tight.

"He's good, picking out college courses after Christmas."

"How wonderful," she said. I handed her the butter. Even her fingers were tense. "I'll leave it on the counter to thaw," she continued. "I'll make them bright in the morning, so they'll stay fresh throughout the day."

"That's a good idea," I said.

I unzipped my coat and kicked off my boots, unintentionally and unavoidably flinging snow onto the tiled floor. Mom walked back into the foyer. "Did you want to watch a movie tonight, Lora?"

And now it was my turn to be tense. I planned on cracking open *Holes* by Louis Sachar. I read it once in grade school and enjoyed Sachar's writing and the story, so I wanted to give it a reread.

"Maybe tomorrow night," I said. "I wanted to get some reading in."

"Oh, alright. Well, at least have a slice of cake before going up to your room, yeah?"

"Of course."

We sat back down at the table with the empty seat, and kept ignoring its emptiness, as Mom sliced the cake and placed the triangles onto tea plates. The deep brown was frosted in white and it reminded me of the snow outside, the frozen earth blanketed in stark downy. I waited to eat my piece until Mom and Dad both had theirs set in front of them. It was delicious.

"This is such a classic," I told Mom.

"Thank you, Lora."

We took our bites and enjoyed the chocolate in silence. The only noise was the sound of each other's chewing.

"Your phone went off a couple more times when you were gone," said Mom.

"Okay," I replied. "I'll check it later."

With every forkful the triangles became shapeless until there was nothing left. I helped clean up, said thank you, and excused myself to my room for the night, but not until after grabbing my phone.

I rushed up the stairs, no longer having the strength to push against curiosity and the manic gestures it can make one do. I closed the door behind me and settled crisscross-applesauce onto my bed in front of my duffle bag. My thumb pushed the center button and the rectangle screen lit up.

There were two messages from an unrecognized number. I clicked on the conversation:

*UNKNOWN: HEY. IT'S HARPER.*

*Unknown: CAN I CALL YOU?*

## 29

Harper's voice sounded different on the phone, deeper almost, as if his vocal cords stretched with the passed minutes from the time I said bye in the hallway to now.

"So, are we good enough friends to earn myself a contact name?"

"Maybe." I smiled to myself. His wit threw me off my feet more times than I'd like to admit.

"Also, sorry if you don't like talking on a phone," he said. "I'm not much of a texter."

"You say sorry a lot," I said.

"I know," he replied. "I'm sorry."

We both laughed at the irony.

"So, did you have something to tell me?" I asked.

"Oh yes, the whole point of me contacting you—therapy schedule." I adjusted my position so that I was lying on my back, staring at the yellow-tinged popcorn ceiling. My lamp coated the tiny bumps in butter. "Sessions start this Thursday. To work with my school schedule they start at 10 a.m. and go to 11 a.m. because I have evening classes. I have to go once a week for three months. By February, I'm a free bird, although I'll have to go once a month after that until they think I don't need it anymore."

"Technically mid-February, right? Since we are already halfway through November?"

"Correct, Ms. Lora."

"Oh, just call me Lora," I said.

"I will, I was just trying to be funny, lighten the mood," said Harper.

"Sorry," I said. "My sense of humour kind of sucks."

"No worries. I can work with that," he said. "So how does that work with your schedule? Do you think you'll be able to come with me?"

"It actually works perfectly. I have evening classes as well Thursdays, and I can ask my boss to have that day off work."

"Oh." Unspoken words haunted the end of those two letters.

"Oh?" I questioned. "Is something wrong?"

"No, it's nothing."

"It doesn't sound like nothing," I said. "Tell me what's wrong Harper."

"I just don't want you going out of your way, Lora. You've already done so much for me."

"It's really no big deal. I can work other days."

"Are you sure?"

"Positive," I replied.

"Thank you, Lora."

"You're welcome, Harper."

"I really appreciate it," he said. "Your being here." Maybe it was the serious turn the conversation took. Maybe it was the gratitude dripping from his voice. Maybe it was all of the above mixed with his deep tone, but his voice sounded like a cello—his words a melody that resonated in my chest. First, it started in my stomach, this fuzzy, fizzy, bubbly sort of feeling. But now it had migrated to my chest and it made me want to laugh, but it also made it hard to breathe. Maybe I could laugh until it became hard to breathe.

"Lora?"

"Yeah?"

"You didn't say anything, I was just making sure you were still there," said Harper.

"Sorry about that." I couldn't possibly tell him that he was giving me what I thought was a good dose of butterflies. I never felt butterflies before...

"So, do you visit your family every weekend?"

I almost forgot that Harper was still on the phone. "No, I'm just helping with some things. We are moving at the end of the month."

"Oh really? Where to?"

"Just another area of Niagara. My parents found a house on the lake that they wouldn't pass up."

"Makes sense. It will make you feel like you're camping every day, with that lakeside view."

*That's exactly what my parents said,* I thought. "Maybe, we'll see."

"You don't sound too thrilled," said Harper.

"I'm not, really," I said.

"May I ask why?"

"It's a long story," I said. Too long of a story.

"Alright, I won't pry," he said. *Good,* I thought, because I didn't even know him yet.

"What about you?" I asked. "Where do you live?"

"On campus," he said matter-of-factly.

"Well, obviously," I said through laughter. "I live on campus, too. But I meant your family, where does your family live?"

All I could hear was Harper's staccato breaths mixed with static. For a second I thought the line had dropped. I took my phone away from my ear to put it in front of my face and checked the screen. The time was still rolling, and the line was still connected, but Harper had stopped talking.

"Harper?"

No response.

"Harper, are you okay?"

Worry crept up on me like a plague, barely noticeable at first, but then all at once my chest grew tighter and tighter. I almost hung up to call back. Maybe he had fallen asleep.

"I'm fine. Meet me at my building, Thursday at 10:30. See you then. Goodnight, Lora."

"Goodnight," I said.

But my words were heard by no one because by the time I had the chance to say them, Harper had already hung up.

**30**

---

I woke up with a stale taste coating my tongue from my disregarded words of last night. My sleep was terrible. I tossed and turned well into the morning, cringed when I checked the time to read that it was 4:00 a.m. and went back to sleep.

Sitting up in bed, I could tell Mom had started baking by the clatter barking from the kitchen and from the smell of a fresh batch of cookies wafting into my room. I always wished there was a way to capture the smell, to stuff it in a jar, only to twist the lid open slightly every time I needed the comfort of home.

I walked into the bathroom to brush my hair and wash my face then walked down into the kitchen.

Flour was scattered in patches across the countertop and twelve golden-brown circles were cooling on a rack. Mom was making another dozen and moulded the balls with spoons, only to flatten them once the dough met the parchment paper. Mangled grunts climbed over the clatter from the dining hall. Dad was busy placing fabric protectors on the chairs.

"Hello, sunshine," he said when he noticed I was watching him. "Slept in a bit, eh?"

"Yeah, sorry."

"No need to apologize, your mom has all your clothes packed away already anyway." He stuck his tongue out, his usual gesture of focus. "This is the last one. Mom didn't make breakfast because of the cookies, but she did lay out some bagels. You could butter one up or put jam on it."

"Thanks, Dad," I said.

I walked back into the kitchen and found the plate of bagels: cinnamon raisin, garlic, and three-cheese. I chose cinnamon raisin and plopped in the toaster for three minutes.

"Good morning, love," said Mom, planting a kiss on my cheek. "How did you sleep?"

"Okay," I said.

"And how did the reading go?" she asked. This was her way of passive-aggressively telling me, "By the way, I know you weren't reading because I could hear you talking aloud to yourself when I went to use the washroom."

"I ended up falling asleep," I said.

"Really? Why are you feeling so tired?" She sounded concerned.

"Mom, I think every university student is tired and needs a nap at least once a day." She didn't seem convinced and continued to stare at me.

"Have you been using moisturizer? I have some that I could give you. It's supposed to brighten your skin."

"Are you trying to tell me I'm ugly?" I asked.

"Lora," she gawked, as if *she* were the one who should be offended. "Of course not. I just want to encourage healthy hygiene."

"Well, don't worry Mom. I use deodorant and brush my teeth twice a day." I knew this was her way of taking care of me, but sometimes her way stung.

The bagel popped out of the toaster, and I grabbed a plate from the cabinet. Instead of butter, I drizzled each circle with some honey, careful not to get any in the hole. I capped the teddy-bear bottle and put it back in the Lazy Suzy.

"Honey," said Mom. "I never thought about that. I should try it some time."

"Deirdre introduced it to me," I said.

I took a seat at one of the bar stools that overlooked the kitchen and watched Mom perform her baking choreography. Now it was time to clean up, with three dozen cookies prepped to be put in the oven.

"You made a lot," I said between bites.

"You'll need the energy, trust me. I also made some sandwiches too, so we can pull those out when we're hungry for lunch."

"You're so prepared," I said. I took a few more sweet bites. "So, what are we doing with the furniture?"

"We are leaving it here for the new family."

It hurt to swallow. "What? Why?"

"Your dad and I decided to purchase more modern furniture since the appliances in the new house are more up-to-date as well. Also, this family is just starting off and they need all the help they can get. How do you feel about leather?"

"I guess it's okay," I said. "So we are leaving our appliances as well?"

"Yes."

"What about the TV?" I asked.

"Of course we are taking the TV, darling."

"Okay, just making sure," I said. "What about our beds?"

"Oh, we ordered those new too."

I didn't feel hungry anymore. I was going into the new place with even less familiarity than I expected. "What about the mattresses?"

"Also new. We got you a queen size, is that okay?"

"Yes," I said. And no. There's nothing wrong with my double bed. There's nothing wrong with our fabric sofa and armchair. "Did you also buy new dressers too?"

"Yes," she said.

"What about the kitchen table?" I asked.

"That's coming with us," said Mom.

I took the last bites, nibbling around the hole. I rinsed my plate in the sink and set it in the dishwasher. "I'm going to go get changed and cleaned up," I said. "Where are we starting first?"

"Well, your room is basically done, and your dad and I will get the little things when it comes closer to moving date, but we wanted to start with the shelves in the family room, get all the picture frames and books into boxes. Our room is done as well."

"You're already living out of boxes?" I asked.

"Like you said, I'm prepared."

"What needs to be done after the family room?"

"Well, we'll put all the taped boxes into the garage and then, I guess, we'll clean out Will's room."

William's room, I wanted to correct her. I always hated when she shortened his name, the four letters instead of seven.

I noticed the hitch in her voice and went upstairs.

**31**

   —

One thing I appreciated most about showers is that they were the perfect place to cry—tears blended with the stream of water, and you didn't have to give an explanation for the red blotches on your skin because the hot water was to blame. If a sob escaped your lips no one would hear it because it would drown in the sound of water hitting the bottom of the tub.

I didn't cry often because when I did, I wouldn't stop.

I cried when I washed my hair. I cried when I rinsed it. I cried when I soaped my body. I cried when I rinsed it too. I cried when I applied conditioner and scrunched my hair. I continued to cry when I shut off the water and wiped the mirror with my towel. I was still crying when I dried off my body and slipped into a long-sleeved sweater and jeans because I couldn't face "cleaning out Will's room." I couldn't grasp the idea. I only stepped foot into his room once after he died, for one of the showings. Mom told me to grab his football jersey so his teammates could sign it. Even then, I thought the walls would start caving in and I ran in and out as fast as possible

I only stopped crying when I brushed my hair because I knew I had to go downstairs to help my parents. I sat on the toilet until I thought five minutes had passed to give my skin time to relax and to regain proper breathing.

I opened the bathroom door, and the steam followed me into the hallway—misty fog—where I opened the closet door and dropped the towel into a laundry basket. I then went to my room and folded my clothes, putting them back into my duffle bag, not a drawer. I checked my phone to find a missed call from an anonymous number—Harper. I rolled my eyes and left the notification. I didn't want to talk to him while I was still upset and hurting. I didn't want to say the wrong thing, and I didn't want to think about how last night went, so I left my phone on my bed.

When I walked back down the hallway and down the stairs, the steam had dissipated and what I was about to face didn't seem too daunting anymore. My parents already packed things into boxes I saw as I made my way into the family room.

"I thought the shower swallowed you, or did the warm water feel too good to get out?" Dad teased.

"It was the warm water," I said.

"Those boxes are filled," Dad said, jabbing his finger in three different directions. The flaps looked like they wanted to fly away. "Would you mind taping them? The tape is on the coffee table."

I took the thick spool of clear tape and I grabbed a pair of scissors from the kitchen. Dad does this magic trick where he can break off pieces with his teeth, but I could never get the hang of it, so I stuck to the easy snips of scissors.

"Wow, do you remember this day?" Mom said to Dad. "Our first camping trip with the kids."

I leaned over her shoulder to take a look at the picture frame Mom was holding and my heart dropped, the heavy muscle sat atop my diaphragm. My breaths came in severed rushes. It was painful.

We were all smiling in front of the lake: Dad and Mom in the back and me and William in front. Except William was holding a giant fish he had just caught, and I looked obnoxiously disgusted by the dead creature. I remembered how Dad skinned and barbecued it that night and I remembered how I threw a tantrum because I didn't "want to eat the fishy!" Mom ended up making me some chicken fingers instead. But William looked so proud holding the fish that was half his size. I wondered where he conjured the strength to hold the creature.

"William was so happy, and I was too," said Dad. "I remember how he squealed when he felt the first tug on the rod, 'I got it, Daddy! I got it!' I had to remind him to keep a firm grip or else he would have lost it to his excitement."

We all laughed, but I knew that inside each of us were crying for the boy holding the giant fish.

"Who would like some cookies?" asked Mom. "Tea or coffee anyone?"

Dad and I both took her up on her offer, but Dad chose coffee and I chose tea.

We had a little snack break at the dining table that would, luckily, be coming with us to the new house, and then we went back to work. Soon the entertainment piece shelves were emptied, as well as the cabinets. We also managed to pack away all of our VHSs and

CDs, excluding one Disney movie that Mom wanted us to watch tonight, my favourite, *The Little Mermaid*.

By the time everything was packed, boxes were taped and everything was moved into the garage, it was time for a late lunch.

We ate more cookies alongside our turkey sandwiches. I felt like we were eating in slow motion, like everyone was taking extra time with every bite, not swallowing until the food had completely dissolved in our mouths, because we weren't looking forward to what we had to do next. I knew I couldn't face it, but I had to for Mom and Dad, because if I broke down and Mom and Dad broke down then the new family would be left with a fully garnished room of a dead boy.

We cleared the plates and placed them in the dishwasher while finishing our last sips of tea and coffee.

We walked up the stairs in silence and stopped in front of the door that mirrored mine. A wooden W used to hang on the outside of the white door but Dad took it down because it hurt too much to look at. I used to have a wooden L on my door too, but I told Dad to take it down because I was too old for it. He took mine down the same day he took down William's.

My hand met the cold, gold surface, and I wanted to back away; tingles already crawled up my elbow and moved to my shoulder. I turned the knob to the right and flicked the switch. The overhead fixture buzzed to life and we were met with the truth of reality that we were so desperately trying to shove from memory:

Loss.

## 32

"Are we keeping anything?" I asked, still standing in the doorway. My parents stood still behind me, not making an effort to push me forward into the room.

"Just his trophies and his teddy bear," said Dad. "Everything else we are donating to Goodwill."

I walked in a little further to see if my parents would follow. "And his bed? Is it staying, except for the mattress?"

"No, that's going too," said Mom.

No one wanted to sleep in a dead person's bed, good shape or not.

I walked in even further, touching the foot of his bed. This time Dad followed, but Mom was stuck in the doorway. Her hand grasped her neck. I imagined she was reliving that day—the day she came home and found an unimaginable nightmare, only this one didn't end when she woke up, it only became more vivid with open eyes. And I stared into her eyes now. They were void of light—spaced out.

Dad opened the tall dresser and started throwing clothes into a pile on the ground. By the time the mound was up to his knees and the drawers were emptied, he was crying, his face red, and Mom collapsed against the doorframe. Silent tears rolled down the hills of her cheeks.

There are no words to describe loss, no words to say how it feels. I could say it felt like an arm was missing, I could say it felt like there was a hole in my chest, a constant aching. I could say it felt like a part of me died too, but none of those thoughts did the pain justice.

We reacted in different ways to loss. Some of us shut down for hours, days or months to become empty vessels, while others felt angry all the time and became violent. Mom—the empty vessel. Dad—full of anger. I didn't know what to call myself.

"Dad," I said. "Why don't you and Mom go relax in your bedroom, and I'll deal with this."

I was a commander.

"Lora," he said wiping at his face, "that's completely unfair to you."

"Dad, trust me. I know someone I can call who will be willing to help me."

I was a problem-solver.

"Okay…" he whispered.

He placed Mom's arms around his neck and lifted her up. He carried her in his arms. When I heard their bedroom door close, I rushed into my room and grabbed my phone. Still ignoring the missed call, I scoured through my contacts, praying I still had what I was looking for. I almost yelped when I found it.

I called Seth.

He picked up on the second ring.

"Hi, Lora?"

"Seth, I need you to help me with something."

I was the foundation of the family when Mom and Dad couldn't be. Even though I too wanted to cry, I did what I had to do to keep this family from falling irreparably apart.

## 33

———

When the doorbell rang, I was inside William's closet, placing all of his shoes into a bin.

I hurried down the stairs and gulped two quick breaths before opening the door.

"Hi," I said in a rush. "Thanks so much for coming. I'm sorry if you had homework or anything."

Seth wrestled me into a hug.

"Nothing that I can't do tomorrow, just some math questions."

"Oh, I'm sorry."

I was quite anxious when it came to school and liked to get things done well before the due date.

"Lora, it's fine. Trust me. I wouldn't be here if I didn't think I could catch up on homework," said Seth.

"I really appreciate it," I said. "Would you like something to eat, drink? Mom made cookies."

"Well, you know how much I've missed your mom's baking, so how could I say no to that?"

He followed me into the kitchen, and I placed three cookies onto a plate for him.

"Speaking of which," he said. "Where are the parentals?"

"I told them to take some time, that I would deal with the room."

"Oh." Seth took a bite of a cookie and looked down at his place. His throat struggled to push down the clump of food.

"Yeah, they—they just…broke down…kind of…" I didn't know how to word it without making my parents seem unstable, because they weren't, they just lived everyday hurting.

"I understand," he said. He looked up into my eyes. "And how are you dealing with all of this?"

I bit my lip. "I'm fine."

"Really, Lora?"

"Really, Seth. I'm fine. Would you like any tea or coffee?"

"A glass of milk will do," he said.

I picked out a glass from the cupboard and grabbed the carton from the fridge, filling the cup halfway. "Mom will be ordering pizza later. You're welcome to stay," I said. "I told my parents how we ran into each other at the store, and they'd love to have you for dinner."

"I'd like that. Thanks," he said.

When he finished the cookies, I took the plate from him and placed it in the sink. I then handed him the cup of milk, which he chugged in seconds, and placed the glass in the sink as well.

"Lead the way," he said, arm extended.

He followed me up the stairs and I could feel his hesitancy permeating into the air, slowing my limbs and hammering my heart. My feet felt heavier with each step, but maybe I was just imagining it all and *I* was the one who was hesitant.

With the door already opened, I freely walked into the clutter and chaos. Dad's pile of clothes still remained an untouched, disgruntled mess and the bin of shoes was swimming in the soles of ones I had yet to pack away.

"The only things we are keeping are his trophies and teddy bear, everything else is being donated."

"Okay," said Seth. He got right down to it. "What would you like me to do with this pile of clothes?" He stared at it like it was a monster, as if it would grow arms and legs and start chasing after him.

"Down the stairs and to the left is the laundry room. On the shelf above the washer and dryer, there are black garbage bags, you can bring the entire box up. The clothes can go into one of those."

He shot me a thumbs-up and left the room. By the time he came back and opened the new box and a garbage bag, I had the entire closet floor packed away. I snapped the lid onto the pin and pushed it into the hallway.

"And now the rest of the closet," I said.

I mimicked Dad and one-by-one threw each article of clothing from its hanger onto the floor. I also made a pile of hangers for Mom and Dad to pack for the move. Hangers always seemed to disappear, and you could never have too many. The pile soon too became quite monstrous and I grabbed one of the black bags, opened it, and started showing clothes inside. Seth had his tied up and put it on top of the shoe bin in the hallway.

"What next?" he asked.

"You can clean out his night table," I said. "All of that can go in the garbage though."

It took three bags to pack away all of William's clothes from the closet. He tended to hoard unnecessary pants and shirts from when he was in grade school because he said they had, "sentimental value," and "you never know when I'll need a tie-died shirt."

I tossed each bag into the hallway, adding to the bulk. Pretty soon no one would be able to walk through and Mom and Dad would be trapped in their room.

When I walked back into William's room, I had to stop and lean against the doorframe. It was empty. The drawers were left open, as were the closet doors, and for the first time since last year it looked like no one had lived here. No more clothes tucked away and even the mattress was stripped of its quilt, sheets and pillows, shoved into a black bag never to be seen again.

I took another garbage bag out of the box and started on his desk. When I opened the cupboard, a hoard of papers fell out and I shoved them in the bag by the fistfuls. Seth told me he was done with the night table and added the bag to the pile in the hallway.

"Want me to help you with the desk?" Seth asked. "Looks quite messy."

"Yes, but first, could you check to make sure there's nothing under the bed?"

He got down on his hands and knees to look under the bed. He fanned his arm left and right and said he didn't feel anything. He then checked the foot of the bed and found a bouncy ball. He handed me the rubber sphere of blue and green, and I chucked it in my garbage bag. He then went around to the side, scanning the carpet.

"Lora, I think you're going to want to come look at this."

*Mom, Dad, Lora, I don't want you to feel guilty, like this was your fault—what I did. I just couldn't be here anymore. I felt like I was a heavy weight, and I wanted to take that weight off of you and everyone I know. I still love you and that will never change. Don't cry over me. Go on with your lives as if I were never here. It's just something I had to do, and I'm sorry if it caused you pain.*

*- William*

When Seth called me over, I kneeled down next to him, but after reading the entire letter, I collapsed onto the floor. My knees met my forehead. I rolled my head back and forth on my knobby bones trying to make sense of it all. Mom and Dad never found a letter. They said there was no explanation. The paper must have fallen off the bed in the hysteria when Mom found him.

I told myself I wouldn't cry, so I didn't. I grabbed the piece of paper from Seth's hands. He was shaking.

"What are you going to do with it?" Seth asked.

I walked out of William's room and into mine. I folded the piece of paper and tucked it into my duffle bag.

He followed me. "Aren't you going to show your parents?" he asked.

"No, Seth. They don't need to see this. It will only make things worse. They couldn't clean out William's room, and that was before a note."

"But, Lora, they should still know."

Ryan Jones

"Please, Seth, I am begging you, drop it, okay?"

"Okay," he said.

"Thank you."

"So," he continued. "What exactly are you going to do with it?"

"I don't know," I said. "As long as Mom and Dad don't find it, that's all that matters, so it'll probably be coming back to school with me." I zipped my duffle bag closed. "Come on, let's go make sure everything is cleaned out."

We walked back into William's room and put stray garbage bags into the hallway. The door across the hall creaked open and out stepped Mom and Dad. Even though they had changed into jeans and sweaters, it was easy to tell that they had been in pjs due to chaotic bedhead.

Mom squinted her eyes. "Seth! It's so nice to see you." She wrapped him in a hug.

"It's nice to see you too," said Seth.

"It's been too long," said Dad, who patted him on the shoulder.

"Lora, what time is it?" Mom turned her squinting eyes to me. I checked my watch.

"It's about five," I said.

"Goodness, we slept much too long," chuckled Mom. "Seth, you will be joining us for dinner, won't you?"

"I already invited him, Mom," I said.

"Oh, good, well, I'll head downstairs and order some pizza."

"That sounds great, Mom," I said.

"Lora and Seth, can you help your dad pack the garbage bags into the car? We'll drop them off tonight. "

"Or," said Seth, "we could pack them in my car, if it's easier on you and everything. Lora and I can bring them to donation while waiting for the pizza to arrive."

"Lora, are you okay with that?" asked Dad.

"I'm more than okay," I said.

Mom mouthed "thank you," to me and headed down the stairs, with Dad in tow, fisting two of the black bags.

I climbed back up the stairs to make sure we didn't leave anything behind.

All that was left was a line of trophies sitting on the desk, and a faded brown teddy bear lying on a white mattress.

**34**
___

I had never been with Seth in a car before. When William and I had hung out with him, we were too young to drive, so we'd just walk or bike everywhere. This was a new feeling.

"Do you know where it is?" I asked.

"Yeah," he said. "I've been a couple times with my mom when she does her spring cleaning. It's on a little road off of the highway."

That's where we were: flying down the highway. Driving always made me uneasy when other people were doing it. I didn't like not having control of the wheel.

Within ten minutes, Seth had us backed into the parking lot, hatch popped, ready to unpack. Seth opened the door to the building and the lady with grey hair behind the counter gave us a warm smile.

"You can place your donations over there," she said, pointing to the side of the room marked with an arrow: Donations Here.

Back and forth we went from the car to buildings. I think it took about five trips to get everything inside. The lady thanked us and told us to have a good night.

When we got back in the car, I checked my watch.

"Do we have time?" asked Seth.

"Time?" I was confused.

"Yeah, do we have time to kill?" he asked again. He still didn't make an effort to take his foot off the break. We were still at a standstill.

"Why?" I asked.

"Want to walk the paths?"

I smiled. It was hard to believe Seth still remembered the place when I myself had long forgotten. If someone brought them up, I would know what they were talking about, but I'd never suggest trekking them again.

"Sure," I said.

He finally took his foot off the break, switched it to gas, and we were on our way.

When we got there it all came back to me—the memories, even the painful ones.

The paths consist of several paths that ran rapidly through a portion of forest; it was like a game of snakes and ladders, and sometimes, you'd fall down the ladder. William, Seth, and I often came here in the summer. One time, we took our bikes, which was a bad idea because William ended up wiping out, head over handlebars.

The bumpy dirt wasn't good for bikes, but it didn't stop him from taking mini-hikes. We'd pack a backpack of snacks as if we were real adventurers out in the wilderness: canned goods, dried goods, granola bars and such. We wouldn't stop walking until we hit the cliff, which opened into a beautiful view of part of the lake. The whole walk took about an hour, and we would sit on a log for another hour, taking in all that was wonderful about Mother Nature.

One time we stayed too late though, and realized the stars were glittering on the lake's surface. We had gotten in a lot of trouble.

We got out of the car and the snow crunched beneath my feet.

"It's just as I remember it," I said. "Only whiter and smaller."

Because everything looks bigger when you're a kid.

"Remember William's wipeout?" asked Seth, closing the driver's side door and locking the car.

"I was actually just thinking about that," I said.

"And remember when there was a snake on the path, and you freaked out?"

*Luckily there weren't any snakes in the winter*, I told myself. "Don't remind me," I told him.

"But it was quite hilarious. I do recall you jumping on your brother's back."

"There's nothing wrong with being scared of snakes," I said. Seth's boots crunched the snow too as we made our way into the woods. "Besides, it's a completely normal fear. Do you have a flashlight? It's getting dark."

Seth took out a small blue one from his pocket. "It was in the center console. It's better than nothing."

We followed the tiny yolk of light as we walked down the narrow path. Seth went before me, so I was able to match his footprints.

"How is school going?" he asked over his shoulder.

"It's good," I said. "I like all my classes, not so much my teachers, but I can't complain."

"Do you have any friends?" he asked.

The emphasis he placed on friends told me he was implying the more than friendly type. "Friends?"

"Yeah," he said. "Any dates, flings, crushes?"

"Seth, we are not close enough to be talking about this," I said.

"But we used to be, Lora," he said.

My chest tightened. "No, I don't have any flings or crushes, but it's none of your business anyway."

"Will you tell me," he asked, "if you do?"

"If I do what?"

"Get a boyfriend… or girlfriend, if that's what you're into."

I laughed. "Seth, please stop."

"I'm being serious, Lora," he said.

"Why?" I asked. "Why do I have to tell you? Why do you need to know if I'm in a relationship?"

"Because," he said, turning to face me, "William would have wanted to know if he were here, but he's not here, so that leaves me, unless you'd rather tell your parents first."

"No, I'll tell you," I said. And I meant it.

"Thank you," he said.

My sides stopped cramping, and we started walking again. We arrived at the log that sat on the cliff which overlooked the lake and damn, was it ever beautiful. The water had frozen in soft waves and the tips were sprinkled in snow.

Seth brushed off the layer of snow that sat on the log and motioned for me to sit next to him, so I did. Our butts pressed against the cold wood and our arms leaned against each other.

"I miss this, you know," he said.

"Yeah," I sighed. "I know."

I knew. I knew that this log was meant to sit three people. I knew. I knew that it used to sit three people, and I also knew that it felt horribly empty only seating two.

I knew that this used to be my favourite place, but it isn't so much anymore because it only reminds me of the person we lost.

## 35

We walked back in silence. I wondered if Seth was thinking of William too.

When we got in the car, Seth blasted the heat. I pressed my hands together and blew my breath into the spaces between my fingers, thawing my skin. Soon, we were back on the highway, 15 minutes from home. The pizza might have beaten us there.

"So how are you with...you know, William? How have you been coping?" I asked.

"You know," he said, "no one has ever asked me that. My parents don't talk about it. I think they try to ignore it because they don't want me to end up like him." He realized how badly his words may have come across. "Sorry."

"Don't be," I said. "If I was in your position my parents would be the same way."

"But I'm okay, I guess," he said. "Some days are harder than others. Some days require a best friend and it sucks that I don't really have one anymore. Of course, I talk to people, but I've never been as close with anyone as I was with William."

"I get it."

In a way, William was my best friend too, being my only sibling. I didn't realize how much I enjoyed having a brother until I didn't have one anymore.

"My parents ignore it, too, I think," I said. "They don't talk about him at all. They've never gone into his room. Today was the first time and they couldn't do it. I understand, but at the same time it sucks that they act like nothing ever happened."

"I'm sorry, Lora," said Seth.

"Sorry? For what?"

"Well, I guess I'm apologizing for life, and how shitty it can be."

"We're all dealt a deck with a few shitty cards," I said.

"Yeah, I guess you're right," he said.

Snow began to cloud the streetlights. It looked like a winter wonderland. It was the soft and fluffy type. I could tell from the flakes' shape and size. The road began to shine.

Five minutes later, Seth parked his SUV in the driveway and we dusted off a layer of snow that had accumulated on our coats walking from the car to the front door. Mom and Dad met us in the foyer.

"Just in time," said Mom. "The pizza just got here, and we have the VHS player all setup. It's a Disney night, Seth, I hope you don't mind. Lora chose *The Little Mermaid*."

"That always was your favourite one," said Seth.

He smiled and handed me his coat which I hung in the hallway closet next to mine.

By the time the movie ended, I had eaten six slices of pizza. Seth told me he was, "rather impressed."

We walked him to the front door with a container of leftover pizza in hand. After putting on his coat and boots Mom gave him a hug.

"Don't be a stranger. Come over any time."

"It was nice seeing you, kiddo," said Dad.

"Text me when you get home," I said, slowly closing the door. "And thank you for all your help today."

"I'm glad I was able to come," he said, walking down the stoop. "And, Lora," he said, turning around. Particles of snow landed on his nose. "If you ever need anything, I'm only a phone call away."

I would have liked to blame the moisture in my eyes on the snowfall, but it was dry inside.

"Thank you," I told him. "Same goes to you."

Something terrible rolled itself into a ball of pain in my chest as I watched him walk to his car, open the door and sit in the driver's seat. It felt like a stone had lodged between two of my ribs and every time I exhaled it hurt so badly that I wanted to cry. I looked behind me to make sure Mom and Dad were no longer in the foyer. They weren't. I was in the clear to let the burning and the pain overtake me, to tuck me under its covers and call it a night. When I heard the engine of his SUV growl to life I just about broke, just about collapsed to my knees in a sobbing mess as I allowed stray tears to trickle down my face, because I didn't know when I'd see him again.

Seth.

Once so close he knew my favourite food, and now so far away that I had found it difficult to confide in him, to open up.

I climbed the stairs and closed my bedroom door behind me, not looking across the hall. I sat on my bed and cried—the silent type. It's so loud that you can't even hear it, only a faint ringing in the ears.

I opened my duffle bag and pulled out the folded note and read it again.

*I just couldn't be here anymore.*

But you could have, I thought, if only you had told me what was going on.

*I felt like I was a heavyweight…*

You were light as air.

*I still love you.*

I do too.

*Don't cry over me.*

Well that, William, is an impossibility.

**36**
———

When I woke up, I noticed my jeans were stuck to my skin and the hoodie I wore was making me sweat. It was also difficult to breathe through the paper which must have landed on my face upon falling asleep. I prayed Mom didn't check on me, but if she had, she would have woken me up and demanded that I explain the note, no matter the time of night.

I rolled over and glanced at my phone. It was 9:30 a.m. with no missed calls or texts from Harper, but one from Seth saying he had gotten home safely. My heart dropped, and I hoped Harper wasn't hurt about me ignoring him. I hoped he hadn't decided to give up on…whatever this was. Friendship?

I stripped out of my sweaty clothes and picked out a clean pair from my duffle bag: another pair of jeans and a yellow turtleneck. I folded the dirty pair and stuffed them into the tight roll of a bag, also tucking the note into one of its pockets. I threw on a pair of wooly socks, quickly applied deodorant and spritzed myself with perfume, hoping all would cover the remnants of restless sleep. I twisted my hair into a knot atop my head and headed downstairs.

Spices of nutmeg and cinnamon invaded my nose. I was worried that a line of drool would end up dripping from my mouth.

"Good morning sunshine," said Dad, sipping his coffee and reading a book at the bar counter. No protection padding for chairs today.

"Good morning," I replied.

I grabbed three mugs from the cabinet and poured coffee into each one, setting all three in our spots on the table. William never drank coffee. I wondered if that would have changed as he got older.

I prepared my coffee first, only cream, and chugged half of it.

"It's that kind of morning?" asked Dad.

"Yep," I said.

I took two rolls and two strips of French toast and powdered the strips with icing sugar. I then placed slices of mango and banana on top.

I took my first bite of French toast and felt the dough being dissolved by the acidic juices of the mango.

"Is there a certain time you'd like to be back to campus?" asked Dad. He took a sip of coffee and looked at me, waiting for my answer.

I swallowed. "Not really," I said. "I don't have too much going on."

He took another sip of coffee but continued to stare at the table this time. "Your mom and I were thinking of visiting the cemetery in the afternoon, once you're packed and ready to go. Then we'll take you back for the evening." I heard him take a hopeful, deep breath. "What do you think about that?" he asked.

I cut one of the French toast strips in half and played with it. "Do we have to?"

"Mom thought it would be nice," he said. "Especially when you haven't visited him in a while."

He was right. The last time I went to his grave was the day before I left for school at the end of August, and now, it was nearing December. I was either an awful sister or unashamedly human, hiding from something I'd rather not face.

"Sure, we can go," I said.

"So," said Mom. "We will be moving about the second week of December. Did you want to help, or did you want to wait till Christmas to see the finished product?"

"Probably Christmas time," I replied after swallowing my bite. "I'll be done with school then, but before that I'll be swamped with final assignments and exams. Is that okay?"

"Of course," said Mom. "Whatever is easier on you, focus on school."

"I'd also like to work more hours before going home for Christmas too."

"That wouldn't hurt," said Dad.

Eventually, the cups were emptied and the plates were cleared and I climbed the stairs to my bedroom to make sure I had everything accounted for: duffle bag, backpack, note, headphones.

I grabbed my phone and texted Seth, apologizing for not getting back to him sooner and said, "I fell asleep." A few minutes later he replied back to me and said it was no big deal and wished me safe travels back to Toronto. I told him thank you and that it was really nice seeing him again, that he should come visit me on campus sometime. He said that maybe one day he will. One day.

I exited out of Seth's conversation and clicked on Harper's.

*Harper: Lora, I'm extremely sorry for being snippy the other night. You didn't deserve it, and I'm sorry if it hurt you. Please let me know when you get this.*

No matter how mad or upset I wanted to be, even through text this boy wouldn't let me be—I felt my cheeks rise.

*Apology accepted.* I texted back.

He replied right away.

*Harper: Are you back yet?*

*I thought you didn't like texting.* I messaged.

*Harper: I don't. But I figured you wouldn't want to talk to me on the phone with how the last one ended.*

He figured correctly.

*It's appreciated.* I texted.

*Harper: Are you back on campus?*

A knock from my bedroom door forced me to look up. It was Mom. "Are you ready?" she asked, looking at my bags sitting at the foot of my bed.

"Yes," I said.

"Looks like it," she replied. "Come on."

She left the doorway, and I looked back at my phone, replying to Harper, *Not yet. Gotta go.*

I twisted my arms through the straps of my backpack and grabbed my duffle bag, pausing at the open door to make sure I wasn't forgetting anything. My feet stuck to the floor, wedged in place, as my eyes roved over every inch of my bedroom—this is it. This will no longer be my bedroom.

I said goodbye to the desk I used to sit, colour, and write at. I said goodbye to the bed I used to pee in when I was transitioning from Pull-Ups to underwear. I said goodbye to the closet that watched me grow up, getting filled and emptied with every other birthday and growth spurt. I said goodbye to it all.

I turned around and was met with a closed door to the room across the hallway. I walked across and opened it, saying goodbye to it too—its emptiness—and the person who used to inhabit it.

I met my parents in the foyer. They already had their coats on, and Mom had a scarf wound around her neck.

"Are you ready?" asked Dad.

"Yes," I said. I shoved my phone into the butt pocket of jeans.

"Alright, let's go," said Dad.

*Let's go,* I told myself, reminding my feet to move. Dad helped me place my duffle bag in the hatch again and I brought my backpack with me into the back seat.

As Dad put the key into the ignition and started to back out the driveway, I said my last goodbye to the burning bricks that would forever be a flame in memory.

Their flames flicked back at me.

That day, I said goodbye to who I was, and soon enough, I'd find who I was meant to become.

## 37

The grave was thirty minutes away, so I pulled out my Mp3 player from the side pouch of my backpack, not really feeling in the mood for conversation. William's tombstone sat in the lawn next to the church we grew up attending.

In went one earbud and then another. I clicked on my Elton John playlist and pressed the shuffle button.

*It's a little bit funny, this feeling inside*
*I'm not one of those who can easily hide*
*I don't have much money, but boy if I did*
*I'd buy a big house where we both could live*

I often wondered where I'd end up after school. My dream was to become a well-known author, but I knew that chasing it wasn't just reaching for the stars—that was like trying to fit the whole universe inside my palm. There was no way all the orbs and planets would fit into the cove; dustings of pixie dust were bound to spill over.

I never wanted to own a house. I always planned to have an apartment, two-bedroomed, one for me and one for a walk-in library, though rent was daunting in the city.

My mind grew tired of my dream chasing and big thoughts, so I closed my eyes and let the headphones block out the world.

They didn't block out the world for long.

Dad reached over the centre console and shook my leg. "Hey, Lora, we're here."

I stopped the playlist and wound my headphones around the small device, putting it back inside its side pouch. I took my mittens out of my backpack and shoved my hands into each. My mittened fingers grasped the handle and I pulled it forward, opening the door into the cold and stray flurries.

Dad opened the black-rod gate that enclosed the cemetery and allowed Mom and I to walk through first. It was freezing.

A fresh bouquet of roses was leaning against one of the headstones—a beacon of red in the setting of white and greys. It gave me comfort seeing the fresh petals. The edges had yet to blacken and shrivel.

We walked away from the other footprints, towards the newer portion. I followed Mom and stopped beside her in front of a tombstone that was nestled underneath a tree.

The words that were etched into the flecked stone bore a hole into my head until I was brave enough to read them:

William Bryant Grayson

August 2, 1990 - September 25, 2007

*Not even two decades*, I thought to myself. I also thought about how we forgot to bring flowers, but I kept it to myself because Mom was already crying, leaning into Dad. I made a mental note to bring a bouquet of daisies once the weather cleared.

I'd often heard parents say how much they hated seeing their children cry, but I thought it was worse the other way around. As a child, you see your parents as these solid, impenetrable structures that let nothing through their doors and windows. When my parents cried, it reminded me that nothing, no one, was safe from feeling.

I stared at the stone poking up from the snow because if I so much as glanced at my parents, I knew I'd turn into a sobbing mess. I started counting the flakes that fell from the sky, landing on the sleeves of my coat, only to melt after a few minutes of sitting on the fabric.

I found it interesting how authentic each snowflake was, a multitude of spikes and legs that Mother Nature melded so carefully together. It stunned me how fast it all melted—the white framework.

I raised my face to the dense clouds and allowed the particles to touch my face. I refrained from sticking my tongue out and catching them on my tongue, but it was tempting. William and I used to do it all the time when we were little. The first snowfall was the most exciting because usually the snow stayed until the end of winter and we knew it was snowman season. Mom would bundle us in snow pants, coats, boots, hats and scarves and we'd play for hours outside. We'd only stop for dinner and hot chocolate. Mom was peeved when we wouldn't come in at night and we continued to play under the streetlights until she started counting down from tten. We never heard her reach below five because if we did, we knew we'd be in a whole heap of trouble.

A wail from Mom racked my body and pulled me out from inside myself. The cold started poking through my coat. I shivered, unable to tell if it was the sound of my mom's cries or the frigid temperatures that made my body shake. The sun fell lower and lower from the sky, becoming more tired every few minutes and the clouds grew darker and darker.

"Darling," said Dad. Tears slicked his face. He looked shiny in the saddest of ways. "It's getting cold and the snow is picking up, we should get going."

"I-I don't want to leave him," said Mom.

My eyelids start to tingle.

It took the efforts of both me and my dad to drag Mom back to SUV with linked arms to help her into the front seat. Dad handed her a package of tissues from the side of the door and she tore them open before I could even get inside the vehicle.

## 38

I fell asleep again on the ride to campus. My heart was heavy and my head pulsated. Even though I wanted to sleep, I knew what I really needed. When I got back to my dorm and said bye to my parents, I told Deirdre I was heading to Starbucks for a bit to get some writing in.

"Alright," she said.

It was oddly quiet in the coffee shop that night, as if everyone in the city had the same plan: avoid the snow.

There was a young girl with brunette hair at the other side of the shop facing the window in an identical bar seat as mine. Her laptop was open, headphones plugged in, a mug sitting next to her. Her fingers poked through the handle, snugly grasping the ceramic—the air above it swirling in clouds of steam.

Another boy with blonde hair and a turtleneck, which reminded me of the one I was wearing, sat at a table of four. He took up the whole space with an array of textbooks spread out and opened. I watched him to see if the fissure between his brows would disappear, but his focus persisted.

Two old men shared a table for two, each of their noses stuck into the folds of newspapers: *The Toronto Star*. One had a full head of hair while the other had none. The one with the full head of hair had a curling moustache and the one with no hair had a scruffy beard. They licked their fingers before turning a page.

I turned back around to face my document and checked the time: 7:00 p.m. I told myself I'd stay for about an hour and then head back.

My fingers didn't fly over the keys like they usually did because I was at a standstill with the storyline. Instead, my fingers hovered, waiting for my brain to do something. I stared at the tiny, black words and I stared at the empty space floating beneath them. Nothing came to me. I took a sip of tea, that was still a bit too hot to drink, and winced.

My phone screen illuminated with a number—Harper's number. I had yet to make him a contact.

"Hello?" I said, accepting the call.

"Hi, Lora, how are you?"

"Who starts a conversation like that these days?" I asked.

"You ask a lot of questions," he said.

"I know," I replied.

"To be fair," he said, "I start many conversations like that, and when I ask how someone is, it's not just an easy way to start a conversation. I genuinely want to know how you're doing. Back in TO?"

"I'm alright, I guess. And yes."

"You guess?"

"Harper," I cut.

"Something seems off about you," he said.

"I'm fine," I said. "Just tired." *I visited my dead brother today.*

"Are you too tired to go for a walk?"

"A walk?" I asked. "It's almost eight o'clock, and it's freezing outside, not to mention it's snowing."

"So that's a hard no for a walk?" he asked.

I didn't respond due to conflicting thoughts and took a sip of tea.

"Hmmm," he said. "What about tomorrow? Do you work?"

"No," I said, putting the cup back on the table. I spun it in circles back and forth with my fingers, "But I have a class in the morning, and I may have to take one of my coworker's shifts."

"Well, plans pending, would you be up for a walk?"

"Where would we be walking to?" I asked.

"Walks don't always have a destination, Lora. Sometimes you need to shut your mind off, let your legs wander. You'll find the best of places that way."

"Not in Toronto," I said. "It's a huge city."

"And we're downtown, so it's perfect," he replied.

Our versions of perfect were a stark contrast—his were grey, for me it was black and white.

"So, let me know when your coworker gets back to you, yeah?" He sounded hopeful.

I couldn't pop his balloon of excitement. "Alright, I will," I said.

"Great, I'll be expecting a text."

"Okay," I said.

My phone coughed when the line ended, and I was left wondering why Harper was so excited.

I shut down my laptop, tucked it into my backpack and bundled up once again.

**39**

———

Arriving back on campus, I hurried to rid myself of the clothes I had worn all day. They made me feel heavy, dark, and dirty, almost as if the dust from the gravestones had accumulated and clung to my coat. It felt like the particles had stuck together and formed a hard casing, slowing my movements. I dried off and got into pjs in the nick of time.

Harper was calling me.

"One minute, I'll just be out in the hall," I told Deirdre while picking up the call.

"Hello?"

"Lora!" he exclaimed. "I thought you disappeared. It is now 10:45 and you still have yet to give me an answer. Am I really that horrid to be around?"

"No problem," he said. "Okay, so, walk tomorrow?"

"Looks like it's a go. I don't need to cover my coworker's shift."

"Excellent! What time are your classes done?"

"I should be done in the late afternoon."

"I'm done around 1 p.m., but I'll just chill at a Starbucks or something until you're done. Sounds good?"

"Yes," I said.

"So just text me and let me know when you're done, and I'll meet you at your building or something,"

"Okay," I said.

I thought he was going to hang up, but he didn't seem quite ready. Silence flooded the line, the type that told me he had something to say, he just didn't know how to say it.

"Harper?" I asked.

Another river of silence broke the conversation and continued to flow for an awkward minute. There must have been a dam down the stream, because the quiet ended when his words crackled through the speaker.

"You know, Lora," he began, "I haven't known you long, and the moments we talk aren't long either, but it seems as though every minute that includes you are the best parts of my day."

His words slammed against the dam that I thought was sturdy and broke every brick. It was my turn to be silent. I had no clue how to respond.

"Anyway," he said. "I wish you sweet dreams. Goodnight, Lora."

"Goodnight, Harper," I responded because that's all I could manage.

"I'm looking forward to tomorrow."

## 40

I slept in and then walked to the campus cafe to pick up a coffee.

Marchie's face lit up at my appearance. "Lora! How are you? Did you have a good time with your family on the weekend?"

"I did, thank you Marchie. How are you? I hope it wasn't too busy without me."

"Not at all. Malcolm and Gemma did just fine, but I'm thinking about hiring a new girl for some extra help for the season. Her name is Hailey. Seems like a good kid. She's a first-year business student."

"Sounds like she'd be a great help," I said.

"So, what can I get you this morning?" asked Marchie.

"Just a large earl grey," I said.

"Not a problem," said Marchie. She started boiling the water and placed a large paper cup on the counter.

"Marchie, can I talk to you about something?" I asked.

"Sure," she said. She placed the teabag in the cup and turned around to face me.

"I was wondering if I could change my availability a bit. Would it be okay if I didn't work on Thursdays anymore? I kind of have these recurrent morning appointments."

"Appointments?" Her glasses lifted with her eyebrows. "Are you feeling okay?" she asked.

"Yes," I said. "I'm fine, it's not for me, it's for a friend."

"Alright," she said. "Not a problem. I'll write it in my notebook when I'm done here."

"Thank you," I said.

The kettle started whistling and she poured the water into the cup, leaving a little room for milk.

"Here you go darling, have a good day."

"Thank you," I said. "You, too."

\*\*\*

Mr. Murphy was early today and was already sitting at the front of the room at his desk. I took my usual spot next to Ophelia, feeling guilty that the teacher arrived before me. I wasn't late, but I liked to arrive early to seem punctual.

"You're a bit later than usual," said Ophelia as I discarded my winter garments and sat down.

"I know," I said. "I slept in."

Everyone stopped talking when Mr. Murphy stood up and walked to the front of the classroom.

"Good morning everyone," he said. "Happy Monday." A few people groaned in response to his cheerfulness. "A lot of you have been emailing me about your progress, and I appreciate that. Today I'm going to take turns with each of you for some one-on-one time to discuss your novel. When your turn is up, you can either choose to stay and work, or if you have other plans, you may leave. The choice is yours. But be respectful and keep the noise level to a

152

minimum, as I would like to hear what your peers have to say. Anyway, happy writing everyone."

I decided to edit a few chapters, and then start writing. I was halfway through the chunk when Mr. Murphy called on me. With the laptop in hand, I walked to the front of the classroom and sat in the chair beside him.

"So, Lora, how's the writing coming?" he asked.

"Pretty well," I said. "I've reached 50K words."

"Wow, good for you, I am impressed. You're well on your way for so early in the game. Now, the last time I checked in with you I stopped revising at chapter thirty. How many more chapters have you written?" he asked.

"I'm at chapter 40 now, sir," I said.

"That's great progress since last week," he said. "May I take a look?"

I placed my laptop in front of him on his desk and let his eyes scour my words, hoping he wasn't judging too harshly.

I always hated when people would read my work. In high school, William often demanded that I let him read what I was working on. I would deny his demands several times, but he eventually softened me by making me laugh and I ended up turning the computer screen around so he could read my words. Whether it was a short story or poetry, even if it needed some chiseling, which many of my works did, he'd still be supportive and say, "I could read that over and over again, Lora."

I stared at the other students and wondered what they were working on. I didn't know them enough to venture guesses; the only person I made friends with in this room was Ophelia.

"I'm impressed," said Mr. Murphy.

I was dragged back to reality. "Oh?"

"You've taken and used a lot of the critiques that both the students, and I have offered you and the story is developing really well. I quite admire your style of writing too."

"Thank you," I said, blushing. My cheeks were hot, and pools of sweat-soaked my palms. I rubbed them back and forth across my jeans, against my flexed thighs that were still trying to keep my body in place.

"I did make a few little notes though," he said. "Or rather, one important one." I nodded my head. "I just want you to work more on scene-setting," he said. "I love all your details, especially the efforts you put into characters, but try to do that more when a character enters a location. Tell us what the character sees, feels, hears and smells. You know what I mean?"

"I do," I said.

"Great."

He spun my laptop around to face me and lifted it up, offering it for me to take. "Thank you," I said.

My cheeks were warm and tingly from smiling.

## 41

When class ended, I pulled off my gloves and texted Harper.

*Hey, I'm done with class,* I said. I checked the time: 2:15 p.m.

He responded right away.

*Harper: Super.*

I waited a few moments to see if he would say anything else. When I didn't receive another text, I sent a question mark.

*Harper: Sorry. Just talking with some of my friends.*

*It's okay,* I replied. *Where do you want to meet?*

*Harper: I was thinking I could meet you where you're at and we could take the subway together to Front Street.*

I shuffled in my spot. *Why Front Street?*

*Harper: You'll see. So, where are you?*

I told him what building I was at and that I'd be waiting outside for him.

*Harper: Okay. See you soon.*

I shoved my phone in my pocket, not trusting my hands. They jerked with nerves, and I knew that I'd end up dropping the device. I shoved my hands back inside my gloves, hoping to halt the anxious tick, and stuck my hat on top of my head. I climbed the stairs and opened the door, leaning against the brick wall and hoping that Harper wouldn't take too long—that he wasn't too far away.

I turned so that my right shoulder was bearing my weight against the wall. The edges of the nude bricks provided little comfort, cutting through the plush feathers of my coat. Stretching my neck, I lifted my face up to the sky and realized it was another cloudy day.

Stray flakes started to dot the campus, dancing in the gentle breeze. I wished that I was one of them—free-spirited.

"Why do you look so serious? You look like you're thinking about something."

I was so far inside myself that I failed to realize Harper had arrived and stood next to me, analyzing my face, my body. His eyes went up and down, then up and down again, only to go up once more. He stared at my face.

"You can't just walk up to people like that; you'll startle them." But it wasn't shock that shook my heart—that clenched my chest.

"You get this line right there," he said, pointing a mitten finger between both my eyebrows, "when you get into deep thought." The fabric of his mittens grazed my skin and I just about melted, a snowflake touching sunlit cement. I wished I could blend into the bricks and melt away.

"So," I said.

"So," he replied. "What are you thinking about?"

"Snowflakes."

"Snowflakes?" He scrunched his face. "You are such a random human being, Lora."

He started walking away from me and it was my cue to follow him.

"Do you know where we're going?" I asked. Even though I went to school in Toronto, I didn't know the city well, only keeping to the roads around campus.

"Of course I do. Faith, trust, and pixie dust. The entrance to the subway is just around the corner."

I walked beside him, hands shoved in pockets, the odd snowflake kissing my skin. After two more blocks, we descended a cement staircase, the hustle of foot traffic and screeching metal penetrated my ears. To some, it was annoying, but to me, I always appreciated the frenzied subway atmosphere.

I jostled around in the side pocket of my backpack, taking out my wallet and TTC pass. I scanned it in front of the metal detector and the plastic doors opened for me to walk through. Harper did the same and we began our way down a tiled set of steps until we reached the St. George platform.

A subway must have just left the station. As soon as we reached the platform, a gust of stale air engulfed us and forced me to place both of my hands on either side of my hat to keep it in place. Harper looked at me and started to chuckle.

"What?" I asked, raising my voice over the echoes of the underground tunnel.

"Nothing," he said, looking at the tiled walls. The smirk didn't leave his face.

His hands were also shoved inside his pockets and I took in the rosiness of his cheeks as the echoes quieted. I stepped a bit closer to him.

"What did I do that was so funny?"

He shrugged his shoulders. "You don't have to *do* anything. You just simply *are*."

"Are what?" I asked.

"Lora," he replied.

I was about to demand that he explain his riddle-like words when the roar of metal grating metal interrupted our conversation. Another gust of wind overtook the people standing on the platform, some turning away for protection from its might, while others turned into it, greeting the metallic smell of the air.

I was one of the people who turned away. Harper was one of the few who turned towards it.

I didn't face the cars of the subway until the wheels came to a stop and Harper tugged my arm, urging me to follow him between the sliding doors and into red, felt-covered seats. He chose the ones that were sideways, so when the car started moving, I had a clear vision of the windows and its various blurred pictures.

For the majority of the ride, all I could see was darkness, but when we stopped at different stations, it was like analyzing different ecosystems. Museum Station, the one right after St. George, was my favourite. It was like watching a movie set in ancient Egypt, with its gold and blue-themed paintings of Pharaoh heads and pyramids.

I didn't find anything spectacular about the other stations, just a change in tile colour, and when the subway stopped at Union

Station a whole flood of people bounded through the doors carrying duffle bags and suitcases, adding even more colour.

I analyzed the glowing map above the doors, the yellows, reds and greens leaving floating galaxies in my vision. When I heard the subway operator say King Station, I grabbed hold of the rod next to the door. When it stopped, Harper and I were the only ones who got out, and a mom and her child took our seats.

We climbed another set of tiled stairs. The smell of damp snow clung to the air as we walked through the plastic doors, spitting us out somewhere onto King Street. The flurries had turned into a steadfast fall in the 30 minutes it took to travel from one station to the next.

"This weather is perfect," said Harper. He was standing on the sidewalk against a building, not making a motion to move.

"You like the snow?" I asked.

"Yes," he said. "Do you?"

"Of course," I replied. "So, is this what we are going to do? Watch the snow fall?"

"Of course not," said Harper. "This is merely a stop along the way."

I wondered how this boy could have such zest for life when only a month ago I had found him depleted of all motivation. He turned right and I followed him. We didn't walk very far before we turned down a cobblestone side street lined with little cafes—holes burrowed into the brick walls of buildings. Harper stopped in front of one halfway down the street and I read the sign: Balzacs.

"That's kind of a funny name," I said.

"Oh, but just wait till you try something off the menu. This cafe is my favourite."

He opened the door for me and I walked inside.

It wasn't terribly spacious, but it didn't need to be—the closeness of the tables and chairs made me feel cozy, like someone had slipped a wool sweater over my head. The chocolate-brown, wrought wood chairs, the toasted bricks that made up the walls, and the heavy scent of coffee made me never want to leave this place. Balzacs mustn't have been a favourite for many, or at least, not during the afternoon. An older couple was reading books near a window seat—table for two, and there was a younger couple who looked like they were on a date, snuggling close at the bar stools. Aside from the intimate couples, no one else occupied the space.

A lady behind the counter greeted us with a warm smile, almost as toasty as the atmosphere. "Welcome to Balzacs," she said. "How can I help you?"

I followed Harper as he inched closer to the cash register while reading the chalkboard menus. I looked at the lady and read her name tag: Rachel. Rachel looked like she was growing impatient and I was about to ask Harper if he was going to order when he started talking.

"We'll take two large hot chocolates," he said.

"Anything else?" Rachel asked.

"No thank you," said Harper.

I had my wallet in hand, prepared to help pay for the drinks, but Harper extended a purple ten-dollar bill over the counter before I had a chance to say anything. Harper shuffled down to the bar.

160

I sidled next to him. "You didn't have to do that," I said. "I was going to pay for mine."

"It's just hot chocolate, Lora," he said.

The tenderness of his brown eyes made me feel uncomfortable, accompanied with his genuine smile, because his words held one meaning while his mannerisms held another:

It wasn't *just* hot chocolate.

**42**
———

The coffee cups were distinguished, void of colour, displaying black and white, so that the white letters of Balzacs stood out, bold and clear.

The warmth seeped through the paper, which then seeped through my gloves, making my hands resilient against the cold. I thought we were going to set up shop inside the café, but Harper thanked the lady and opened the door for me. I walked outside and fluffy pom-poms bounced off my coat.

"Where to?" I asked.

"First," he said, "you have to take a sip."

"But it's piping hot," I said.

"I need you take a sip," he said. I thought his eager smile would make his face explode.

"Fine." Carefully, I placed the black lip of the lid to my mouth and slowly leaned backward, waiting for the creamy liquid to enter my mouth without burning my tongue. A couple drops sat atop my tongue—all I would allow. Even the small amount was scalding, but when I tasted it and swallowed, I was thoroughly impressed. My cheeks perked.

"So?" questioned Harper.

"It's good," I said. "Really good."

"Better than anything Starbucks can whip up, right?"

"Starbucks is pretty good," I said, "but Balzacs is slightly better."

I was impressed how he kept his cup sturdy in one hand while he fist-pumped the air with the other. I was also inspired by his enjoyment from little things.

We kept walking a little ways until we entered a small park outlined with a black wrought-iron fence. There was a white gazebo to the left, blending with the snow, a frozen pond in the centre, and an array of trees all around, giving the tranquil park privacy from the busy city. Harper walked to a bench that was facing the frozen pond and dusted off the thin layer of snow that had started to accumulate. The bench was sectioned into thirds, divided with two black iron arm rests. He took one third, and I took another next to him.

Even though the armrest was cold, I was grateful for the separation it offered; I wasn't prepared to be so close to Harper. He leaned his right arm on top of our shared armrest and took a sip of his hot chocolate.

"So," he started, "I feel like I have some explaining to do."

The drink was still too hot but I took a sip anyway, hoping the creaminess would ease my nerves. "Oh?"

"For the other day," he said. "Or, I should say, the other night… when I kinda snapped at you."

"Oh," I said.

He took another sip of his hot chocolate, and I listened as he swallowed the liquid. The cold metal was pressing against my jeans, firing goosebumps on my skin, but I tried to ignore it. I wanted to hang on to his every word and not let go.

"Family is a touchy subject for me because I've never really had one."

"Oh," I said again. "I'm so sorry, Harper, if I knew I never would have brought it up…"

He cut me off. "You have nothing to apologize for, Lora. How I acted is entirely on me. You don't know my past. You didn't know the subject would be a trigger. I just need to learn to handle my emotions better. I really, really suck at it."

I pressed my fingers against one another inside my gloves, trying rub away that sweat that was forming. "We can all, at times, let our emotions get the best of us."

"But mine are so much more than that," he said, "than getting the best of me—because they bring out the worst in me. They consume me until I feel like there's no reason to fight anymore."

He stopped to squint at the sky. Some snowflakes landed in his eyelashes and I wanted to blow them away. "I guess I've never really had a reason to fight, because I've had no one to fight for, no one who has stuck around enough to care. You're really lucky, Lora, having the parents you do. I can tell they care about you by the fact that you slot off weekends to visit them. I don't have that."

"They aren't always the greatest," I chuckled, trying to ease the weight of this conversation, but it only seemed to get heavier.

"I don't even know who my birth parents are," said Harper. "Growing up, I bounced around from foster home to foster home. I could never stay in one place for more than a year because I'd always act out, and eventually, the couple would have enough. The social worker would pick me up and take me away to a different home, only for the same thing to happen again and again."

"I'm so sorry, Harper." The paper cup wasn't as warm anymore, it stopped pulsating through my gloves, and when I took a sip of the hot chocolate, I realized it had gone cold.

"I used to get bullied by the older siblings in many families. They'd tell me I wasn't wanted, that I'd never be wanted, because not even my own parents wanted me. It may seem dumb, but it really got to me, especially over the years. Makes you feel worthless.

"I made some really good friends in high school and kept part time jobs. Once I was 18 and graduated, I moved away to Toronto with some of my friends. We split rent, and I kept working until I had enough money to pay for school. I didn't get to start right out of high school, but it was worth having the money."

"I can understand," I said. "I didn't start right after high school either."

He turned and looked at me—his eyes were the only warmth on this winter day. "How old are you, Lora?"

"20," I said.

Harper replied, "What made you wait 2 years?"

"That's a story for another time," I said.

"Well, then maybe we can do this again," he said. "Only the next time, it's your turn to tell a story."

"Yeah…maybe." I pushed back the sleeve of my coat and checked my watch. It was 4 p.m.

"Do you have somewhere to be?" he asked.

"No," I said. "I just like knowing what time it is."

165

"I'm just teasing," he replied. "I should probably head back to campus anyway, Mika is waiting for me to have a mini Star Wars marathon tonight, which will probably consist of him falling asleep halfway through the second movie."

He stood up and wiped particles of snow off the back of his coat. When I stood up, he did the same for me, and I just about fell to my knees. I started to wobble and standing became impossible. I grabbed onto the iron armrest to right myself.

"Are you alright?" he asked. He chugged the rest of his cold hot chocolate and tossed it into the black iron trash bin beside the bench.

"Yes," I said. "Just a head rush." When I was able to stand without holding anything, I also chugged my cold drink and tossed it into the garbage.

It was a short walk back to the station. When we got on the subway, Harper chose a seat above a heater. The backs of my calves felt like were about to burn into pieces of charcoal, but it was okay because I was warm, and I had good company. This time we were sitting backwards, which bugged my stomach, but I distracted myself with conversation and people watching.

"So, do you have any plans tonight?" asked Harper.

"I do not," I replied.

"Do you like Star Wars?" he asked. I pressed my lips together, hoping he wouldn't notice if I didn't answer, afraid of his reaction if I told him the truth. "Lora," he started, "have you never watched Star Wars before?"

He was genuinely shocked, and I laughed at his heaving gasp. "I grew up watching Disney," I said.

"This is blasphemous." For a second I thought he was getting so worked up that he had to take his coat off, but he was struggling to take his phone out of his pocket. "I'm texting Mika to order takeout for three."

"For three?" I asked.

"You're coming over and watching Star Wars with us. There's no way you're not." His fingers were typing furiously. I thought I'd see sparks crackling from the tips.

"I don't want to intrude," I said.

"Oh, it's no intrusion," said Harper. "Mika will demand that you come as well. Everyone should watch Star Wars at least once in their life." Laughter bubbled inside me. His enthusiasm was quite comical.

After getting back to St. George station and back to campus, we made our way towards the opposite dormitory building and it felt weird not walking to my usual building, calling it a night with Deirdre. I'd only popped into Harper's place once for a few minutes—I was nervous to spend actual time there. I kept reminding myself that I didn't really know him.

We were a few feet away from the doors when I took out my phone to text Deirdre and tell her what I was doing for the night, and that hopefully I wouldn't be too late.

Harper opened the door for me again. "How about we take the elevator this time?" His voice followed me inside.

"Okay," I said, even though I wanted to say no. At least with the stairs I could follow behind him, only having to look at his back. In the elevator, I'd be forced to spend a minute too long-standing next to him in silence.

We shuffled our feet across the entrance mat and he walked to the elevator pressing the up arrow, an all-too-familiar gesture. I wondered how many times I'd pressed the same arrow at the hospital.

"After you," said Harper, as the doors started to open.

I walked in first and he quickly followed, his shoulder touching mine. "Thank you," I said.

"Even though I've bounced around many families," said Harper, "the one common thing I learned was to always treat a lady with respect."

His eyes locked on mine, smiling. I was smiling too. My face grew so warm that I became dizzy, and I thought it was because of this warmth and dizziness that it felt like I was tilting forward, but it was *Harper* who was leaning forward.

The doors opened and I scurried into the hallway, thankful to cool down. I stopped and turned around, waiting for Harper to follow. "I forgot where your room is," I said.

"Just keep going straight," he said. "Six doors down on the right."

With each door passed I counted: one, two, three, four, five...

Six.

I stood in front of the toffee brown door, looking at Harper for what to do next. He stepped in front of me and twisted the knob, but it was locked, so he knocked.

"Coming," came a muffled voice through the closed door.

Three clicks sounded through the silence and then the door opened to a smiling Mika. "Lora," he said. "I hear you've never watched Star Wars before, I'm glad you could come."

Harper grazed the small of my back, initiating me to walk forward into the room. The door clicked closed behind me. Harper was the last one to enter.

My phone buzzed so I took it out of my pocket. It was Deirdre.

**Deirdre: So much for staying friends.**

"His roommate Mika is here too," I typed back. "Get those thoughts out of your head."

I put my phone into my butt pocket and Mika told me I could rest my coat and backpack on the bench next to the door. Once my winter garments were off, I bunched my hat, gloves, and scarf into the sleeves of my coat and sat it next to my backpack.

I turned around, taking in the room. I was able to take my time. I guessed that the navy quilted bed closest to the door was Harper's. All the pillows were neatly propped at the head of the bed, the small ones leaning against the big ones, and the quilt was tucked in between the box spring and mattress. It looked strained. Mika was sitting on the other one, black and white bedding pulled halfback to expose his Star Wars bedsheets.

Instead of two desks, they had a seating area set up with a TV and bean bag chairs. Mika had the stack of movies displayed on the small coffee table next to the remote. The TV screen was blue, waiting for the play button to be pressed. They even had a mini-fridge where Mika grabbed everyone a pop.

He handed one to me. "Thank you," I said.

"You're welcome. Choose any seat you'd like."

There was a red bean bag chair, a grey one, and a blue one. I chose the red one because it was closest to the corner, away from the door and the beds. Harper chose the grey one next to mine and Mika sat in the blue one.

"The pizza will take about an hour to get here," said Mika, "But in the meantime we can start watching the first movie."

He hit a button on the remote and the screen started playing previews. I snuggled deeper into the alcove of the bean bag and thought to myself:

*This feels incredibly comfortable.*

My eyes drifted to Harper's smiling face.

## 43

It was Thursday morning, and I was getting ready to grab coffee with Harper before bussing to therapy. *The week went by quickly,* I thought to myself, as I was applying a light layer of mascara to my lashes. Ophelia and I managed to have a writing session, bumping up my word count and I thought about how Mr. Murphy will be pleased.

Monday night memories paused and played in my mind, as I tried not to poke myself in the eye, one of the most painful things a girl could do. It burned more than a finger touching a flame.

I paused, remembering the look on Harper's face: a permanent happy glow that didn't fall from his features all night. Usually, I felt awkward and constrained around strangers, but with Harper and Mika, I didn't—effortless comfort. I joined in with jokes, added opinions to conversations and talked with Mika about different characters in the movie. I kept track of the time on my phone and my stomach dropped further and further as I realized the minutes were inching closer to me leaving.

It was only when I left that the awkward, constraining feeling started to take over because Harper walked me out of the room and down the hall to the elevator. He pressed the button for me and thanked me for a, "lovely evening."

I told him he was the one to thank because he created the plan, and then...

Then he placed each of his hands on each of my shoulders, pulling me close. My chin rested on the top of his right shoulder and my arms were forced to clasp around his neck, as his arms tightened around my torso. Each of our limbs was touching and all I could think was, "I've never been this close to a boy before."

The toes of our shoes bumped against each other, our pelvises permeating warmth, arms intertwined.

When the elevator dinged, I backed away and scurried into the metal box, leaving Harper with a frazzled wave as the doors separated us.

Deirdre knocked on the door and opened it. "Are you almost done?"

"Yes," I said, because I was, despite the daydreaming. Daydreaming wasn't normal for me and I thought about going to the clinic to make sure I was okay. "Just have to put all this away."

I picked up the bottle of my foundation, the tube of eyeliner and mascara, and packed them all into my makeup bag. "You look nice," said Deirdre.

"Thank you," I said, opening the top drawer of my dresser, placing the makeup bag inside.

"Are you going somewhere?" she asked.

"Therapy, remember?"

"Oh, right. Sorry," she said.

"No worries."

"Let me know how it goes," she called from the bathroom.

"I will," I said. "Don't forget that I have an evening class tonight."

"Alright," she said.

I zipped up my coat, shoved my hands into gloves and fitted a pair of earmuffs on my head. I grabbed my purse and rushed out the door.

I was crossing the courtyard, about ten minutes away from the Starbucks, when I received a text message from Harper.

*Harper: You're late.*

I couldn't reply because it was too cold to take my hands out of my gloves. I picked up my pace, trying to avoid patches of ice that patterned the sidewalk.

I managed to avoid the slippery areas and before I knew it, I was walking through the glass, double doors. I removed my gloves to respond to Harper when I bumped into someone. Harper, standing right in front of me.

"Oh, sorry," I said.

"You know, texting and walking can be dangerous," he said, laughing.

"I was responding to you," I said, returning the laughter. He walked up to the cash register and I followed him. "I can pay this time."

"You can," he said, "but you won't."

"Why not?" I asked.

"Because I am."

He ordered two grande pike roasts and quickly slid the coins across the counter. He turned to me, smiling, but the edges of my lips were sinking.

"Why won't you let me pay?" I asked.

173

I followed him to the bar area to wait for the drinks. "Because ladies shouldn't have to pay if a gentleman is around."

"But we're friends, so why can't I pay for myself?"

Harper clenched his teeth, and I noticed three steady pulses push against the sides of his jaw, nostrils flaring. "Alright, Lora, next time I'll let you pay."

"Okay," I said. "Thank you."

The barista placed the two paper cups on top of the flecked counter. I grabbed mine and Harper grabbed his own, following me to the cream and sugar. When we fixed our coffees, popped the lids on and inserted the green stoppers, we made our way to the bus stop that would take us to Harper's therapy session.

We made it to the stop as the bus was rolling along the curb. Harper got on first, swiping his transport pass, and chose two front-facing seats. I joined him, sitting on the blue velvet. Our shoulders touched again, but I made sure to shuffle my feet over, keeping my legs and boots out of his area. Good thing I did: he started incessantly tapping his right heel up and down, jiggling our seats. I was going to take out my Mp3 and listen to music, but the tapping would push through my headphones.

"Are you okay?" I asked.

He was looking out the window and I watched to see if the reflection of his face would change, but there was no twitch of a lip or raising of an eyebrow that signified him hearing me.

I asked again, "Harper, are you okay?"

"Hm?"

He spun his face around to meet mine own and our noses almost brushed—nearly an Eskimo kiss.

"I asked you if you were okay," I said. His right heel persisted with its tap dance against the floor of the bus.

"I'm fine. I just don't really want to do this. It wasn't my choice."

"Is there anything I can do?" I asked.

His gaze floated back to the window but flicked to meet mine after I asked the question. His eyes held mine in place, our heads bobbing with the bumps in the road.

"You're here. That's all I need."

**44**

———

When we reached our stop, I was afraid Harper wouldn't get off the bus. When I pulled the yellow cord to tell the bus driver a stop was requested, he didn't motion to get up—his feet remained planted to the floor and the back of the person's head in front of him must have looked awfully interesting for he kept staring forward.

"Come on, Harper," I said, gently touching his shoulder.

He didn't move.

"Harper, let's go," I urged.

I looped my arm through his and dragged him out of the seat, down the centre aisle and out the side doors.

"Thank you!" I called to the bus driver on the way out.

When our feet hit the sidewalk, I unlinked our arms and stood in front of him.

"Are you sure you're okay?" I asked. "Okay enough to do this?"

The brown building was a few feet behind us—the warm bricks looked inviting, like a cabin that would have a fire going. The chilly air clouded my breaths as I huffed in frustration. He was looking everywhere but at me. I raised my voice to overpower the traffic.

"Harper, please talk to me," I said.

I thought he was going to remain in this frozen state forever, that I'd again have to link my arm through his and walk him to the door, but something inside him must have thawed and his face changed, his eyes meeting mine.

"Yep, let's go," he said.

He had such pep in his step and I was taken off guard, dragging behind him, but I eventually met his pace, jogging for a couple feet. I didn't want to talk in case my words froze something inside him again.

He walked to the building with such confidence, practically throwing the door open. I caught the handle and walked through after him, gently closing it behind me.

A secretary was sitting behind a front desk and her face perked up when she saw us walk into the lobby.

"Hi," she said, smiling. "Are you here for Dr. Montgomery?"

Harper fidgeted in his pockets and produced a small, white business card. He inspected it, brows furrowed. "Yes," he said, looking at the card again to double-check its information.

"She'll just be a couple more minutes," said the secretary. "She's with a client, but feel free to take a seat while you wait."

"Thank you," I said.

I turned towards the lines of seats but turned back around when the secretary spoke again. "Sorry, before you get comfortable, which one of you is Harper Engels?"

"That would be me," said Harper. He took a long stride forward.

"I'll just need you to sign in." The secretary placed a clipboard and pen on top of the counter and told Harper where to sign. He flourished his hand so quickly I thought the pen might snap. "Thank you, Harper," said the secretary. "You may take a seat now."

I led the way, taking a seat in a row of chairs in front of a tall window that faced the secretary. Harper sat right next to me.

"She seemed nice," I said.

"Yeah," he said.

Silence. The humming of the heater vent above us was the only noise, along with the occasional tapping of a keyboard from the secretary.

"Do you know how long it'll be?" I asked.

"Probably around 30 minutes," he replied.

"Okay."

"Okay."

We hit an impasse.

"How are you feeling?" I asked.

That was the worst question that could have come out of my mouth. I stared at him, waiting to see if he would make eye contact. When he eventually did, his face held no expression, and I worried that I said the wrong thing, but after a few more awkward moments of holding each other's eyes, his face started to bubble and a smirk began to creep around his scowl, until he was holding his belly, bent over laughing.

That's when I *knew* I had said that wrong thing.

His face was turning red and he started wheezing, struggling for air.

"Harper," I said. "Cut it out."

But he continued to laugh.

"Come on, Harper, please, it wasn't that funny. In fact, I shouldn't have said it at all."

Eventually he consumed enough air to form words. "It's just so ironic," he choked through fits of giggles, "asking me how I'm feeling while I'm waiting to go into therapy. That was a good one, Lora."

I stared at my shoes. I felt so heavy. I wanted to pull a salt-stained boot off my foot and bang it against my head for being such an idiot with words.

"I'm sorry, Harper, really." I looked over at the secretary, but she didn't seem bothered. Maybe she thought I told a really good joke. I wish I *had* told a really good joke.

"Don't be." He took in a big gulp of air and exhaled loudly. "I needed that laugh to take the edge off. I'm glad you're here."

His face transformed from red to his normal skin tone and I stopped worrying about his health. A door creaked down the hall, followed by the click-clack of heels and a middle-aged woman with black hair and full front bangs met us in the waiting area.

"Hello," she said. "I'm Dr. Montgomery." She extended her hand and we both shook it.

When I imagined a therapist, I expected an older woman or man who'd be impatient, wasting no time. Dr. Montgomery exuded calm and casualness. Instead of dress pants, she wore black denim, and instead of a blazer, she wore a formal top.

"Thank you for coming along, Lora, I appreciate it, and I'm sure Harper does too," said Dr. Montgomery. Harper shot me a side smirk. "Unfortunately, you can't come with us into the room but you're more than welcome to get comfortable. Mandy, the secretary, could get you some coffee or tea while you wait."

"Thank you," I said.

She smiled at both of us. "Harper, shall we?"

She extended her arm so he had a clear walk from the lobby to the hallway. His first few steps were feeble and when he looked at me, I could tell he was scared.

"I'll be right here when you're done," I reminded him.

I watched the backs of Harper and Dr. Montgomery as they walked single file down the hallway until they disappeared.

## 45
---

After a few minutes of sitting alone, the secretary walked over, holding a brown paper cup and a small paper plate of powdered donuts.

"It's black tea," she said, sitting the cup and paper in front of me on the coffee table. "So I added some milk and sugar, is that okay?"

"Yes," I said. "Thank you."

"And there are some donuts in case you get hungry."

She left me with a smile and her heels click-clacked as she made her way back to the desk.

I waited 'til she sat down, until her face disappeared behind the counter, to take a quiet sip of tea and a nibble of a donut. I felt out of place, never being in a therapy centre before, though I almost was...

Mom and Dad ordered me to the kitchen because they told me we needed to have a sit-down conversation. *We* meaning *me*. I could tell by

Dad's crossed arms that he wasn't impressed, and Mom wouldn't sit down. Everything felt uneasy and I grabbed the sides of the cushion of the dining room chair I was sitting on.

I knew what it would be about. After William died, I did nothing. I stayed in my room for a whole week reading books, drinking tea and eating toast, because I didn't want to face the world that waited for me outside my bedroom door.

Mom spoke first. "Lora, if you're going to continue with this behavior, we will have to send you to therapy."

I bit my bottom lip. I wanted to scream. I wanted to get so close in my mom's face so not only could she feel my breath, but smell it as well—the unbrushed scent. "I don't want therapy," I told them, looking them each in the eye. "I will not go."

"Then something needs to change, Lora," said Dad. "You need to go to school, or, at least, get out of your room."

But none of it would be the same anymore. Even breathing wasn't the same without him. But how could I express this without falling apart?

They let me go back to my room after that.

I had cried all night.

I took another sip of tea as a shiver passed over me. I pulled my unzipped coat tighter around my body and waited for it to subside. Being in this building reminded me of the 'could-be's. I could have been like Harper too, scared to walk into the room with Dr. Montgomery.

I finished one of the donuts and took another sip of tea until the cup was half full.

I started to wonder how much time had passed, pulling out my phone, when I heard a door open and a familiar click-clack grew louder...

And louder and louder, until Dr. Montgomery and Harper stood before me. My eyes followed their steps the entire way.

"I'll see you next week," said Dr. Montgomery, dropping Harper off. "It was nice to meet you again, Lora."

"It was nice to meet you, too," I said.

I heard Dr. Montgomery walk away, but I was focused on Harper's face—unreadable.

"Do you want the last donut?" I asked, handing him the paper plate sprinkled with powder.

He took it from my hand and grabbed the donut between his index finger and thumb, shoving the entire circle in his mouth. It was gone in one bite. I tried to hide my laughter while taking the last sips of tea, but a few giggles bounced off the dried paper bottom. The empty cup met the table with a clack, Harper smiled at me.

He took the plate and the cup and threw them in the garbage next to the bookcase, its shelves sprawled with lifestyle and science magazines. He walked back over and started putting on his coat.

"Thank you," I said.

"You're welcome," he replied.

I zipped up my own coat and tingles pricked my skin. When I looked up, I found Harper watching me. My privacy was invaded as he watched me dress. His eyes followed my fingers, riding the zipper all the way up my neck, and I watched his face, wondering about the multitude of thoughts that were spinning around in his mind.

Once I put on my hat and gloves, I cleared my throat. "Are you ready to go?"

I shook him from his daydream. "Um, yes," he said, quickly shoving his hat on his head. "Let's go."

183

The bus ride was silent, and 30 minutes later, we were deposited back at campus. I checked my phone to find that time had moved slower than I expected. It was just reaching one o'clock.

We stood at the bus stop, the snow glistening at our feet from the sun. "What time is your class at?" I asked.

"It's at four," he answered.

"Mine is at five."

"Do you have any plans in the next three hours, Lora?" he asked.

"I don't," I said.

"Would you like to make some plans, with me?" His eyes dropped to the snow only to float back up to my face, finding a smile. He smiled back.

"Sure," I said. "But I should probably grab my backpack and school things from my dorm."

"Okay," said Harper. "Can I accompany you?"

"Sure," I said, because I didn't want him waiting for me in the cold, sunshine or not.

I scanned us into the building and walked to the elevator, hitting the up arrow.

"You may be introduced to my roommate Deirdre," I told him. "Sometimes she pops in for a nap between classes, though I can't remember her schedule today."

"That's okay," he said.

The elevator was taking its time. I found it hard to breathe around Harper and I worried the flapping of my butterfly breaths would be deafening in the silence.

When the doors opened, I didn't waste time and found a spot closest to the buttons, pressing level three. I pushed my back into the back corner and mentally thanked the engineers who built the elevator for not putting in mirrors—I could already feel Harper's prying eyes crawling along my face, I didn't need to look up and find I was right. My shoulder blades pressed against the cool walls.

I broke the silence. "So, what did you have in mind?"

"I thought we could grab another coffee," he said.

"Oh, alright." I was expecting something more because Harper was the type of person who always gave his most.

"You seem disappointed," he said.

"I'm not," I replied. Coffee meant more conversation, more chances for vulnerabilities to be exposed.

"I'll even let you pay for your own this time," he offered.

The doors opened, and I stepped into the hallway, turning around to face Harper. "Okay," I said. "Thank you."

He followed me down the hallway until I stopped out the end, taking off my backpack to fish out the key. When I found it, I stuck it in the hole, turning the gold medal to the left. The door unlatched and I opened it, switching on the main light.

Deirdre hadn't been here since the morning and both of our beds were unmade. I had clothes tumbling out of my laundry basket, reminding me about the trip I needed to take to the laundromat.

I spun around, blocking Harper's path.

"You can't go in there," I said. The words rushed out my mouth.

He looked startled. "What? Why?"

"It's messy," I said. "I haven't had a chance to clean up."

"That doesn't bother me Lora," he said.

"But it bothers me."

"Okay," he replied, "I'll wait in the hallway."

"Thank you," I said.

I didn't want to be rude, so I left the door partly open, a sliver of a crack in case he wanted to talk. I threw my purse onto my bed and grabbed my laptop from my desk, jamming it into my backpack that almost didn't zip.

I jumped forward, almost tripping over a shirt that tangled itself around my boot.

"Looks like you need to do some laundry." Harper's head was poking through the crack in the door.

"Harper!" I ran to the door and slammed it shut, not stopping to worry if I had hurt him.

"I'm fine," he said. "Not like my face was there or anything."

I made sure my backpack was closed and shouldered it, turning off the main light while opening the door.

"I thought you said you were going to stay in the hallway," I said.

My eyebrows set in a hard line. I was unimpressed.

"I was going to ask if you wanted help cleaning up," he said.

I walked to the elevator, not checking to see if he was following me, and hit the down button.

His voice carried over my shoulders and I could feel his breath brush my neck. "So, about that laundry."

"What about it?" I refused to face him.

"Would you like some help?"

The doors opened and I walked in, hitting the button for ground level. I crossed my arms, planting my feet hip-width apart—defiance. "I know how to do laundry, Harper."

"But chores are always nicer when you're doing them with someone."

I didn't say anything and waited for the elevator to stop. When it did, I bustled through the opened doors, out of the lobby and into the cold.

"So how does tomorrow night sound?" he asked.

"I don't know what you mean," I said. With quick shuffles he met me at my side.

"I mean," he replied, "how about tomorrow night I keep you company while you do laundry? Do you work?"

"No," I said.

"Great," he said. "So how about I pick you up around seven?"

I continued walking, not saying a word.

"I'll take that as a yes," he said.

"Okay," I said.

When we reached Starbucks, he held the door open for me. I walked to the register first and ordered and paid for my own coffee. I waited for Harper to do the same and then chose a table.

We settled in one for two next to a wall with a coffee bean portrait. I gently placed my backpack next to my chair and uncapped my coffee to blow on it. I took a sip.

Harper looked at the portrait. Harper looked at me.

"You know, I really hate those pictures," he said.

I choked on laughter. "Why?"

"Because it's too easy. It's obvious. Everyone expects pictures of coffee beans to be displayed in a cafe."

"Isn't that the point?" I asked.

He raised his eyebrows at me. "I prefer originality, pieces that make you look beneath the surface."

His eyes flitted back to the photo of the oversized coffee bean, but I could tell he was talking about more than just the photo.

## 46

I had 20 minutes to spare before Harper arrived.

I scrambled, trying to find as many quarters as I could. I forgot to go to the bank and break a ten-dollar bill so I collected whatever I had in my purse, along with stray change I found around the dorm.

I shoved my hand between my mattress and box spring, finding nothing, but was successful when I sifted through the cupboard of my desk, pulling out two quarters.

Deirdre was laughing as I reached a frazzled state. "I can spot you some change," she said.

I stopped shoving my clothes into a laundry basket and straightened to meet her gaze. "Really?" I asked. "How much do you have on you?"

"I think I have about three dollars in quarters." Deirdre got off her bed and walked to her desk where her purse sat on the chair. Reaching inside, she moved her hand back and forth. She pulled out a fistful of silver coins and handed them to me.

"Thank you," I said.

"No problem," she replied. She crawled back into bed and pulled the sheet over her legs, once again opening her textbook. "It's odd to me," said Deirdre, grabbing her glasses from the night table. She nestled them onto the bridge of her nose.

"What is?" I asked. I was finishing emptying my laundry bin into the basket.

"Harper is going to help you with laundry. Is this like a date?"

"No, Deirdre," I said.

"Seems like it," she replied.

"How so?" I placed the now full basket onto my bed and sat down next to it.

"He's obviously interested in you," she said.

"We're just friends," I reminded her.

"Lora." She plopped her textbook down so that her hands were empty to point at me. "If he were just your friend or had the intentions of being just your friend, he wouldn't spend a Friday night with you at a laundromat. Trust me—boys have better things to do with their time." She stuck her nose back inside her textbook, when my phone buzzed. I checked it—Harper. He was here.

"I have to go," I said.

"Alright, have fun," said Deirdre. "Although, I don't know how much fun you can have with laundry." She smiled at me like she knew just how much fun I could have because she persisted to think there was something more than friendship brewing between Harper and me.

"Thanks," I said. I shoved my purse onto my shoulder and hipped the laundry basket, opening the door and stepping into the hallway.

It took a few minutes to get down to the lobby and outside. When my breath mixed with the frigid air, I was blinded by little clouds billowing out of my mouth.

"Hi."

I almost dropped the laundry basket and I cursed at the thought of my clothes sprawled across the snow. "Harper, you scared me," I said. He was leaning against the building to the right, the door blocking his body.

"Do you need some help with that?" he asked. He grabbed the basket from my hip without waiting for an answer.

"Oh, thank you," I said. I pulled the strap of my purse higher onto my shoulder. "It's not that far of a walk. Just a couple blocks over."

"I know," he said. "Doesn't mean a lady should have to carry heavy objects."

"But it's not heavy," I said.

"Still, I'm with you, so why should you have to carry it?"

I was walking beside him so he couldn't see me roll my eyes. He was so stubborn.

"I *can* do things for myself," I said.

"I know you can," he replied. "But isn't it nice when you don't have to?"

"I suppose so," I said.

Our clouded breaths mixed together in the air, forming a thunderhead of tension. I wanted to know the thoughts in his mind. I wanted to know the feelings of his heart—all that he thought and felt, with me and about me.

My own thoughts went back to Deirdre's words and made me wonder if there was something beneath both of our skins that wanted more.

When we arrived at the laundromat, I opened the door for Harper, letting him walk in first with the basket. He chose a washer and dryer set up in the back corner, away from the expansive windows—eyes to the city.

"Is this okay?" he asked.

"Yes," I said.

I placed my purse on the set of washers and dryers across from the set I was using and emptied out all the change I brought.

"Wow," said Harper. "Do you think you have enough?"

He winked at me. I nearly peed.

"I think I have more than enough." I tried to joke back. "I just like to be prepared."

He set the basket on the floor and started sorting my clothes. I rushed over, and not thinking, grabbed his wrist.

"Woah," I said. "You don't have to do that, really. I don't need you seeing all of my...clothes..." I said. I wanted to say bras and underwear, but I would have blushed too much. Heat was already climbing up my neck just thinking about it.

"Oh, right, sorry," he said. He backed away and leaned against the washer next to us.

"No, it's okay," I said. "There are just some things friends don't need to see."

There was that word again, tumbling with ease out of my mouth: *friends*.

"You're right," he said. "My apologies for overstepping."

I grabbed some quarters from the pile I made and put them into the coin slot. I organized my clothes in whites, colours and darks, and put my whites in the washer first.

"It shouldn't take too long," I said. "The loads are small."

"No big deal to me, I'm in no rush," said Harper. "Cleared my entire agenda just for this."

He started laughing. "I call your bluff," I said. "You don't seem like the type who uses an agenda."

"Very good," he said. "You caught me. I'm not in the slightest. If I need to remember something, I'll jot it down on a sticky note, but that's about it."

"That's okay," I said, punching in the settings. The washing machine whirred to life. "It's better than nothing."

He stepped away from the machine he was leaning on and he looked at the ceiling. "Do you hear that?"

"Do I hear what?" I asked.

It was difficult to make out over the sounds of the wash, mixed with our voices of conversation, but when we both shut our mouths Christmas music filled the space:

*I really can't stay (Baby it's cold outside)*

Hearing the tune made me realize that November was almost over, that my parents would be moving next weekend and my roots would be uplifted.

My hand tightened around the edge of the machine and tried steadying my breaths as my knuckles blended into the white.

"Hey, are you okay?" asked Harper.

He took a few steps toward me and I took a few steps backward. "Yes," I replied. "I just realized this month is almost over."

He stayed where he was. "You don't have to talk about it if you don't want to, but I can tell something is bothering you, and if you'd like to talk about it, I'm here. But, if you don't want to talk about it, I'm here still."

Looking up at him was a bad idea, because when my eyes met his I felt so safe and all the walls I had built around myself came tumbling down. I was a flower without a pot, sticking straight out of the ground for someone to pick.

I started crying.

But instead of ripping me from the ground, Harper tended to and admired the plant. He tugged me into a hug, the type where my arms were pressed against my body, so I couldn't hug him back. He held my head and pressed it to his shoulder, as all the tears left my body.

The longer I cried the tighter he held me.

Eventually, there was nothing left to cry.

"I'm so sorry," I said, wiggling out of his arms. "I'm such a mess. You probably think I'm crazy."

He watched me as I wiped my face with the sleeves of my sweater. "Not at all," he said.

"Sorry," I said again. I leaned back against the washing machine and the vibrations shook me through the denim of my jeans.

"I've never understood the concept of saying sorry for crying," said Harper. "That's like saying sorry for being human."

He shoved his hands in his pocket and walked over to me. He leaned against the washer, beside me. "And for what it's worth, I'm glad I'm here for you. Crying alone is a really shitty thing."

"Yeah," I said. "It really is."

"So don't be sorry, okay?"

I could feel him looking at me so I looked at him too.

"Okay," I said.

And all I could think about? The fact that he was close enough to kiss.

**47**

———

Deirdre had a lot of questions for me that night:

How did it go?

Did you have fun?

Did you kiss?

I was too tired to answer any of them. So I didn't. All I thought about while falling asleep was Harper holding me while crying.

The next morning, I woke up and felt fine. The weekend flew by and I worked double shifts Saturday and Sunday. I didn't complain because it kept me busy and it meant more money.

Eventually Thursday rolled around and I woke up early again. This time I met Harper at Starbucks instead of meeting at one of our dorms.

When I walked through the front doors, he was all smiles.

"Good morning," he said.

"Good morning," I replied.

We didn't talk a whole lot aside from hanging out, just the occasional text or phone call. It felt casual. I liked it that way. Even though I cried in front of him last week, things weren't awkward.

"Can I pay for you?" he asked.

"Why?" I asked.

"Because," he said, "you're the one accompanying *me*, remember? And if you say no it's pointless anyway because I already ordered for you."

"You're impossible," I said, laughing.

We walked to the bar and waited for our coffees. When they were placed on the counter, we brought them over to the other counter that housed the sugar, cream and milk. I twisted open the cream and poured.

"Why do you only put cream in your coffee?" asked Harper. "That seems like it would be disgusting." He used milk and sugar.

"I used to think the same thing," I said, "until I went out for coffee with my friend Ophelia. She told me what she took in her coffee and it changed my world."

"You strange, strange human being." He shook his head but wore a smile. "Maybe I'll try it someday," he said.

"Maybe you will," I replied. "And when you do, make sure you tell me how amazing it is."

"Or how horrible it is."

I laughed. "That too."

He opened the door for me as we entered into the cold. We walked to the bus stop and waited for a few minutes, sipping our coffees, before the hulking vehicle rolled to a stop beside the curb.

Harper walked to the back this time and, again, chose two seats, side-by-side. And, again, he took the window seat.

He didn't tap his heel this time, but he picked his nails.

"You shouldn't do that," I told him. "You'll start a bad habit."

"I know," he said. His words bounced off the window. "Just nervous."

I wanted to say that I was too because tomorrow my parents would start emptying the house of us, transferring boxes to a new and unfamiliar place, but I decided not to because our circumstances were completely different.

I took another sip of coffee.

"You'll be okay," I said. "You did it last week, and you can do it this week too."

"Thanks, Lora."

"You're welcome."

"I'm really glad you're here," he said. Rays of sun were poking through the holes in his brown curls of hair, distracting me from conversation.

"Lora, did you hear what I said?"

"Hm?"

I looked into his eyes. "I asked how you are feeling today," he repeated.

"Oh," I replied. "Fine, I guess."

"Which means something is bothering you," he said.

"Harper, I am okay."

"You sure?" he asked.

"Just have some things going on," I said.

"Do you want to talk about it?" he asked.

"Not really," I said. I didn't want to add weight to his already heavy day.

"If you change your mind, I'm always open," he said.

"I know," I said. "And I really appreciate it."

His hand twitched and I was scared he was going to touch me. I didn't know where his fingers would end up: my arm? My leg? I had never been touched in either place by anyone before.

I was grateful when the bus came to our stop because sitting next to Harper only made my nerves crazier.

We downed the rest of our coffees and threw them in the trash outside the building. We walked into the lobby and the cheery secretary greeted us again. She already had a cup of tea and a plate of donuts prepared for me, sitting on top of the coffee table.

"Thank you," I said.

"You're most welcome," she replied.

I took off my purse and winter coat, settling into a cushioned seat. After Dr. Montgomery retrieved Harper, I pulled out my phone. My finger found the contact I was looking for and pressed the call button.

"Mom?" She picked up on the first ring.

"Hi! Lora, hunny, are you okay?"

"Are you busy?" I asked.

"Things aren't too busy at work. Are you okay?" she asked again.

"I'm fine," I said. "Are you and Dad starting to move things tomorrow?"

"We are," she said.

"Okay," I said.

"Are you sure you don't want to come?" she asked.

"I'm sure," I said. "I just wanted to know when the process would begin."

"Okay. Well I should get back now. I love you, darling."

"Love you, too," I said.

She hung up.

Reality started to sink in, its anchor heavy on my chest. The tea the secretary brought me did little to soothe the anxiety that was starting to claw my chest from the inside out. I was so lost inside myself that when Dr. Montgomery and Harper entered the lobby, I was surprised to find them already talking to me.

She told me how nice it was to see me again, and I told her, "Yes, it was really nice seeing you again too."

I hustled, shrugging on my coat and shouldering my purse. I left the cup on the table, even though there was still tea leftover. I couldn't get out of the building fast enough. My lungs were craving fresh air from the weight they were battling.

Harper quickly followed me. He raised his eyebrows at me in question but said nothing.

We rode the bus in silence and when his gloved hand folded around my mittened one, I didn't protest.

In that moment, I needed him just as much as he needed me.

**48**

———

Harper didn't speak until we were off the bus, walking back to the dorms.

"Hey, so, there's this thing tomorrow night," he started. "It's an art show. A bunch of pictures hung on walls for people to admire, or dislike. Our art teacher invited us so that we could get some, 'inspiration.'"

He scratched the back of his head. "I was wondering if you'd like to come with me," he said. "It's a suit and tie kind of ordeal, so if that bugs you, I completely understand, or if you don't want to come at all, that's okay too."

He was babbling. I found it cute that he was as nervous asking as I was to respond.

"I'd like to go with you, Harper," I replied.

"Really?" He turned and smiled at me.

"Really," I said, returning his smile.

We were in the middle of the courtyard now. I had to go one way and he had to go another.

"Great. It's at Denison Gallery on Wingold Avenue. It starts around 8, but you can come for 8:30 if you'd like."

"Alright," I said.

"So, you'll meet me there?" he asked.

"Absolutely," I replied.

"Great, I'm excited! I'll text you when I'm there," he said.

"And I'll text you when I'm on the way."

"I have to go now and work on a project, but I'm super pumped to see you tomorrow." He started walking backwards and I was afraid he was going to trip from how excited he was.

"Bye, Harper."

"Bye, Lora."

He walked his way, and I walked mine.

When I entered my dorm room Deirdre was sitting at her desk, taking notes from a textbook.

She turned around when she heard the door open and close.

"I think Harper just asked me on a date," I blurted.

## 49

When the next day rolled around, it felt even more like a date as I applied lipstick and eyeliner.

Deirdre was sitting on her bed, waiting for me to step out of the bathroom. She let me borrow a slim, wine-red dress with three-quarter sleeves and a neckline that fell just beneath my collar bone. The dress ended just above my knees.

"Harper will love this," she said. "And you should wear these," she said, handing me a pair of shiny black heels.

I said okay and took the clothes into the bathroom with me. She also reminded me to curl my hair, to give my, "limp, blonde strands some shape." All of this took about an hour, and by the time I was done, it was almost eight o'clock. I wasn't going to be on time.

I unplugged the curling iron and walked out of the bathroom with pegs for heels. Deirdre's jaw dropped.

"Oh, come now," I said. "It's not that great."

"You don't give yourself enough credit," she said. "It looks like you're a model about to strut her first runway."

All I could do was laugh as I stuffed my phone and a few dollar bills into a tiny clutch.

"Want me to call a taxi for you?" asked Deirdre. "You shouldn't be walking in the snow like that."

I hadn't thought about that. "Really? I would appreciate that," I said.

"Don't mention it." She picked up her phone from beside her and gave the driver the address for pickup. When the call ended, she placed her phone back on her bed. "He said he will be here in five minutes. He was already around the area."

"Thank you so much, Deirdre," I said. She got off her bed and stood up to wrap me in a hug. I pulled away after a few seconds. "I'm going to go wait outside, so he doesn't take off without me."

Deirdre laughed. "He won't do that, but I understand the nerves."

"I'll see you later tonight. Just text me when you're going to sleep so I can make sure to be quiet," I told her.

"Alright," she said, nose back in her textbook. "Have fun and be safe."

"Always," I said.

I walked out the door into the hallway, rode the elevator down into the lobby, and walked into the freezing cold where a yellow taxi was already waiting.

**50**

——

My bare legs stuck to the leather seats of the taxi, and I felt uncomfortable sitting alone in the back seat, the only other person in the car being the driver—a stranger. Before this day, I had never driven in a taxi. I had always used transit.

I gave the driver the address and he said he could get me there in 20 minutes. I told him that was perfect and thanked him for driving me, but inside, my bones were rattling against one another. I had 20 minutes to calm my nerves and stop the jitters from sending trembles throughout my limbs. 20 minutes didn't feel like enough, and I started worrying about whether I remembered to put on deodorant.

I focused on the money rate machine that sat next to the driver attached to the dashboard. It glowed red with numbers and it seemed to help. It kept my mind distracted as I said the numbers in my head every time they changed:

$6.00

$7.00

The machine stopped at $15.00 and I realized the vehicle had stopped too. The driver turned around.

"Fifteen dollars ma'am."

I pulled the money from my clutch, and it closed with a click.

"Thank you very much," said the driver.

"You're welcome," I said. I made sure I had everything I brought with me and pulled on the handle, opening the door. "And thank you again."

I closed the door and stood on the damp sidewalk, sprinkled with salt, as I watched the yellow taxi drive away. The tires screeched and I was left in a cloud of fumes. I suddenly felt unsteady in the heels and wished there was a nearby railing to cling onto. Better yet, I wished I had worn flats.

I glanced down the street, first to the right and then to the left. The street looked deserted. There were plenty of businesses, but they all seemed to be closed as no lights were on. All the windows were filled with shadows from the reflections of the lamppost lights in slush puddles. I didn't see the gallery and was about to text Harper about the address when I turned around.

It seemed that all the life on the street had congregated into one building. Outside, the windows were lined with fairy lights, and inside, large, circular chandeliers hung from different sections of the ceiling. They looked like pearls.

Men in black suits crowded the space, as did women in fancy dresses. It was hard to pick out each individual person as they all blended into one blob, like an artist who blended all the colours on a palette.

My eyes floated above the fairy lights and I read the sign. I was in the right place.

Even with this confirmation I was hesitant to enter. The place seemed too grandiose for me. But after a few minutes I scrunched my toes in my heels and stepped forward, opening the door.

As soon as I entered the gallery, an older gentleman offered to take my coat.

"I'll put it in the coat check," he told me. "When you're done for the night, just ask for it."

"Okay," I said. "Thank you."

When I took my coat off and handed it to the gentleman, I felt even more exposed. I looked into the crowd, scanning the faces, hoping I'd find Harper's familiar curls and sharp bone structure.

I didn't, so I opened my clutch and pulled out my phone, checking the time. It was 8:40. I clicked on his message inbox and texted him:

Where are you?

He replied right away.

Harper: I'm at the back. Are you here?!

His excitement made me wobble in my heels. I switched the screen off and placed my phone back into my clutch, closing it.

I weaved my way around groups of people with champagne glasses in their hands and I avoided the ones who were standing in front of paintings. I didn't know how spacious the place was until I finally found the back of the gallery, several minutes later.

The back looked no different than the front or the in-between. The only difference was the paintings. They seemed more playful, less experienced, but still just as beautiful. I looked around and the faces looked younger too—students. But I still didn't see Harper.

Two hands clasped each of my shoulders and my heart jumped into my mouth as I turned around. I swallowed it in a hurry and exhaled when I realized the hands belonged to Harper.

His hands were still resting on each of my shoulders, but he had stepped away to look at me. I felt like one of the pieces hanging on the grey walls.

"I almost didn't recognize you," he said. His eyes were roving my body and I wished the dress wasn't so tight. "You know, with the makeup and all, because you usually don't wear any, which I also like." He tugged me close and squeezed me. "Bottom line, you look amazing. Now, come meet my friends."

He rested his hand on the small of my back and led the way. It was hard to focus on the crowd around me because Harper too looked amazing. His curls were shining with gel and he was sporting a plum purple bow tie, enhancing the brown of his eyes.

"Again, I'm really glad you came," he whispered into my ear. His breath was warm, adding to my increasing body temperature. My stomach was bubbling with butterflies. He pushed me towards a small group. "Mika, Abbie, this is Lora."

Mika looked professional in his dress shirt and blazer. He shook my hand. "Nice seeing you again, Lora."

"You too," I replied.

Abbie stepped forward. She wore a floor-length, strapless, forest green gown. "I've bumped into you briefly at Starbucks, but it's nice to finally be introduced to you." She also wrapped me in a hug. This group seemed like the warm, hugging type. "Harper talks about you all the time."

He cleared his throat behind me, and I felt his fingers tense against my back. "Anyway, I'm going to show Lora around."

Mika and Abbie smiled at us as Harper steered me to the left corner of the room.

"You talk about me?" I asked.

"Just about how you've been helping me," he said.

"Helping you?"

"They know I struggle with depression; they just don't know the gritty details."

"Okay," I said. The crowd started to thin as we edged the gallery. "Are any of these yours?"

We stopped in front of a canvas consisting of blacks and greys. It looked like a warbled person, grabbing their face. Their mouth was opened, screaming between the cracks of fingers, as they kneeled on the ground.

"Harper…" I was mesmerized. "Did you paint this?"

"Mhm."

I looked at him. His mouth was set in a straight line and he was watching me, analyzing my reaction. "This is one of the most beautiful things I have ever seen," I said. Because it was. I was shocked at the amount of talent this boy possessed.

There was watching a sunrise and seeing the pale lavenders of the world mix with the tart peaches in the sky—tranquility. There was squishing your toes in the sand—comfort. There was the smell of a campfire reaching inside your nose on the days of camping—familiarity.

But this was something I had yet to witness. It was as if Harper took the handle of his paintbrush and sharpened it to make an incision down his abdomen, only to crack his ribs wide open, taking his heart out and squishing it against a white canvas.

This was vulnerability.

This was the unveiling of monsters.

But I found Harper's vulnerable monsters to be works of art and I realized that this was what falling in love was: seeing the darkest corners of a person and stepping into the void anyway, candle in hand.

I was falling in love with Harper Lee Engels.

My heart felt like it was on fire, its smoke floating its way to my head. My eyes started burning.

I was afraid it would start pouring out my ears, but the walls of the gallery were grey anyway, and it would blend in.

Harper's painting mixed with my realization left me lightheaded and I leaned into Harper. He placed his finger gingerly around my waist, as if he were unsure if doing so was appropriate.

I didn't say anything, and neither did he. We just leaned into one another, taking in the artwork.

Moments that don't need to be filled with words are the best ones, because that's when you know you're absolutely comfortable with someone: when all you need is their presence, even in the quiet.

Harper and I filled this moment with quiet breaths and the rising and falling of chests. I didn't want to move because I didn't want to pop the intimate bubble that had formed around us. I also found it difficult admitting to myself that I was falling for this lovely boy because everything was already perfect as it was. I decided to keep my revelation silent, tucked into the folds of my own heart.

A gentleman walked near us holding a silver tray. "Champagne?"

I had to blink for a few moments and remind myself where I was. Harper politely accepted for the both of us and handed me a flute. When the gentleman left, Harper turned to me.

"Lora." His eyes were dark, like his painting.

"Yes?"

"Do you trust me?"

"I think I'm starting too."

He offered me his hand, and I took it. I trailed behind him, my hand in his, and he led me to another area in the back.

We arrived at a set of glass double doors. He let go of my hand and pushed on the handle. It opened into a courtyard with benches and dead shrubbery.

I would have been cold in the thin fabric of the dress if it weren't for the closeness of Harper and the sips of champagne.

The door closed behind us, separating us from the rest of reality.

**51**

———

The benches were powdered in snow, so we decided to lean against the brick wall. Harper took off his blazer and placed it around my shoulders. We stood in silence for a few moments while we emptied our flutes. When there was nothing left, Harper placed them atop a bench.

"I'm sorry," he said. "I'm not one for planning. We won't stay out here too long."

"Why are we out here?" I asked. I was afraid to hear his answer.

"Because if people inside heard us talking about how fucked up I am we'd be getting looks left, right and centre."

I nodded because I didn't trust my voice in case it sounded as shaky as I felt.

Harper crossed his arms over his chest and I pulled his jacket tighter around my shoulders. "I almost didn't submit that piece for this show," he said.

"Why?" I asked.

"Because." He kicked a piece of ice with his right shoe. "It's too personal, but my teacher insisted. He said, 'That's the one, Harper. That the one people will stop and look at, that'll make them feel something.' But I was terrified of what they'd feel."

"We're all terrified of our own feelings," I said.

"But that piece is especially scary, Lora. I painted it a week before, you know…"

My breath hitched in my throat and I almost started coughing. "At least it's honest," I managed to say. "I'd rather see someone's tortured mind on display than the colourful veil they use to hide it."

"You do have a point, Lora," he said to me.

"Harper." My breath clouded in the air.

"Lora." His breath clouded too.

They collided.

"Can I ask you something?"

"Anything," he replied. But I thought to myself that he may not want me to ask this one thing.

"Why did you do it?"

He knew what I was talking about because it took him a few moments to answer. "Can I ask *you* something, Lora?"

"Yes," I said.

He cleared his throat. "Have you ever experienced anxiety? Or depression?"

"I have," I replied.

"And do you continue to?" he asked.

"No," I said.

"Good. Because it's a nasty bitch." He sighed. "I'd never seen a doctor or been to therapy before this year, but I knew something wasn't right with me, because I woke up and ached every day, for no reason, and that's no way to live. I didn't know if it was because of my past and the lack of roots it left me for my future, but all I knew is that I walked around with this weight, every day. And each day it just grew heavier and heavier, until it hurt to breathe. So, I wouldn't get out of bed. I fell behind in school which only added to the weight. I woke up one night and told myself I was done living like this, that I'd rather die. So, I took the knife I'd kept under my bed and walked to an alley where no one would find me...but then you did."

Harper's words hollowed my limbs and my heart split open, blood filling the spaces. I was overwhelmed with sadness and tears started streaking my face, digging trails in my foundation, smudging my eyeshadow.

But I didn't care.

As much as I pained for Harper, I also thought about William. I wondered if he too felt heavy to the point of not being able to breathe. I thought about how alone he was, not letting anyone else know how he was feeling, not letting anyone share his weight, to try and lighten the load.

"Hey, Lora, I'm sorry. Please don't cry."

Harper took my face in his hand and turned me towards him. He wiped the tears from my eyes with both of his thumbs.

"I'm so glad I found you," I said through laboured breathing. "Because your life means so much more than the demons you face and your inability to conquer them. No one, and I mean absolutely no one, should have to face that alone."

"You're right," he said.

"Harper." I blinked away my tears so that his face became clearer. "I need you to promise me something." He removed his thumbs from my eyes and clasped his hands around my neck. "Promise me you'll let me lighten the load if you ever feel like you can't carry on, if things ever become too much for you. Promise me you'll let me help you."

"Okay, Lora. I promise."

"Because he never did," I said.

"He?"

"My brother, William. He took his life. Only, he didn't use a blade, he swallowed a whole bottle of pills. And that was it. Gone forever." I was falling apart, but Harper was doing a good job of keeping me together. "I woke up every morning for months wishing it had all been a nightmare. Because it's so sick that when people die, they look like they're sleeping, like you could poke them and their eyes will open. But my mom shook William and held him till her limbs were too tired... and nothing."

"My gosh." Harper pressed me against his chest, tightening his arms around me as I tried to catch my breath. "Lora, I am so, so sorry."

He and I both knew that all the 'sorry's in the world wouldn't stop the ache in people's hearts, but it was nice knowing that someone cared. He cared enough to let me ruin his white dress shirt. It was spotted with black patches of eyeliner.

I pulled away, sniffling. "Oh, Harper, I'm sorry." I pointed at the ruins.

"It's just a shirt, Lora. I can get another one." He stared at me, holding my face between both his hands. "Do you want me to take you home?"

I nodded, my face still soaked in tears even though I stopped crying a few minutes ago.

He pulled out his phone from his pant pocket with one hand still pressed against my face. He must have called for a taxi because he gave the person on the phone our current location and where we needed to go. When he hung up, he shoved the phone back in his pocket and placed his other hand on my cheek again.

"He's 15 minutes away."

He pulled me in close again, and I saw the darkness of the splotches my tears had made on his shirt.

If only people were as replaceable as clothing.

## 52

That night opened a new door between Harper and me.

There was a wall we built between each other that we didn't know existed, but with every word shared, a brick was removed, until there was nothing left but empty air.

And eventually we became comfortable enough to fill the empty air with outstretched hands, and we grabbed hold of each other, not letting go.

So, when exams were complete and the chaos of school simmered, I asked him what he was doing for Christmas break. I was wrapped in my quilt in my dorm, phone pressed against my ear.

"I never have plans," he told me. "Sometimes I'll do things with my friends, but I never leave campus."

"Then come with me," I said.

"Where?" he asked.

"Home," I said. "With me. Come to Niagara with me."

"Really?" he asked. "Your family would be okay with that? You'd be okay with that?"

"I'd be more than okay," I told him. "I just have to ask my family."

So the next day I called Mom and asked her if I could bring a friend home over the Christmas break. I wasn't lying when I called Harper a friend: I didn't really know what we were. We hadn't kissed or anything.

"You said his name was Harper?" she asked. "Why have I never heard of him before?"

"Because we just met this year," I said.

I told her he had no one to spend the holiday season with and that no one should be alone on Christmas. She told me she'd have to talk it over with Dad, but the day after she said it wouldn't be a problem.

So, the next week when Mom and Dad came to pick me up there was an extra person in the car.

"So, what do you study, Harper?" asked Dad.

"Visual arts," he replied.

"Wow, that is fascinating," said Mom. "What got you into art?"

"It was just something I was good at in high school," said Harper.

"You're lucky," said Mom. "That's a rare talent."

There was a lull in conversation as it began to snow. Dad needed to pay extra attention to the road.

"Are you excited to see the new house, Lora?" asked Mom.

Harper looked at me and raised his eyebrows. "New house?"

"Oh, Lora didn't tell you," said Mom. "We moved a few weeks ago. We used to live in a quaint subdivision, but her dad and I felt it was time for a change."

Really, it was just time for them to run away.

"Yeah, sorry," I said. "I forgot to mention that."

"It's okay," said Harper. "Exam week is always crazy."

Mom continued to talk to us about how exams went until there was nothing more to say about the topic. She was satisfied to learn that everything went well and soon all our mouths stopped moving. I leaned my head against the headrest and closed my eyes.

I opened them when I felt someone shaking my shoulder. It was Harper. And for a second I was confused as to why he was in the vehicle, but then I fully woke up and wiped away the fog of sleep, remembering the holiday plans.

"We're here," he said.

I rubbed my eyes then looked out the window. It was hard to see anything through the layer of flakes that clung to the glass. All I could make out was the thick layer of snow that covered the ground.

I pulled on the handle and opened the door. My feet were instantly buried in a casing of snow, which I was grateful for because it kept me steady while facing the new house for the first time.

It was stunning. It looked like it was made for Canadian winters by the way the snow formed a line on top of the rounded logs that formed the walls of the house. It looked like frosting.

The windows were huge and the peaked roof was severe. It looked like a picture from a hiking catalogue, just what my parents wanted.

Dad handed me and Harper our bags and as I was walking up to the house, I noticed there was a wrap-around porch. Mom would love that in the summer, perfect for hosting parties.

But, my favourite thing of all was that the backyard tapered into a lake. At the old house, I had to drive to trails and hike for an hour to see a sight like this. But now? I just had to walk outside.

I stopped on the front steps to admire the view when Harper walked up behind me. "It feels like a campsite," he said.

"Yeah," I replied. "We did a lot of camping when I was little."

"Why do we ever grow up?" asked Harper.

"I don't know," I replied. "Because it's unavoidable?"

I wished I could have stopped the clock during the days of campfire and smores, because growing up could kill a person.

And it did…William.

And it nearly did…Harper.

And I wondered about all the people I didn't know who were affected as well from this thing called growing up. It shouldn't be called that. Because I've seen it take a lot of people down.

My eyes glazed over like the ice on the lake, but Harper pulled me from my reverie. "Come on, Lora. Let's see your new home."

I allowed him to pass me on the steps and I followed behind him.

I was too scared to be the first one to open the door, to see what this portion of growing up would demand of me.

They say that as one door closes, another one opens, but they never tell you how painful it is to close them.

**53**

———

Although, they also never tell you how refreshing opening a door could be.

It was like scraping off the remnants of old nail polish.

Walking through the door, I wasn't reminded of the empty room upstairs, because William had never lived here. I wasn't reminded of loss, because William hadn't been lost here.

He'd never touched these floors or these walls.

Everything was ours.

Everything was new.

The mat at the entrance was rather small and I was worried about getting snow on the shiny, hardwood flooring.

Mom and Dad already took their shoes off, tucking them away in the walk-in closet. Mom walked out. "We'll eventually get a better mat," she said. "One that'll better protect the floors from winter, but in the meantime, I can take your coats for you."

Harper and I dropped our bags on the floor beside the mat and unzipped our coats. We handed them to Mom.

"Thank you," said Harper. He bent down to pick up his bag and he picked up mine too.

I stepped out of my boots, placing them in the closet. Harper stepped out of his too. I walked to the bottom of the stairs and outlined its spiral, reaching the second level. Each step was built with polished wood and a strip of burgundy carpet ran down the middle, ensuring socked feet wouldn't slip.

Since I was already looking up, I went farther with my gaze, tilting my head back. The entire ceiling formed one open expanse, connected by beams and rafters, which were also built out of polished wood. This place was ginormous, and I felt like an ant crawling among the floor of a rainforest.

Mom started walking up the stairs, so I followed, Harper trailing behind me.

"This is a real nice place," he said.

"Thank you," said Mom. "Lora, what do you think so far?"

"Big," I replied, because all I could manage was one word. I was awestruck. I cleared my throat. "Why do we need so much space?"

"It's not necessarily a need, Lora," said Mom. We were still climbing the stairs. "This house has always been a dream for Dad and me, but once we saw it was for sale, it became reality. It was perfect timing."

My hand slid along the caramel wood and we finally reached the second level. To the left was an open sitting area surrounded by railings that overlooked the first level. To the right was a hallway, also lined with a burgundy rug.

"There's no basement," said Mom. She waited for us to join her in the sitting area. She leaned against the railing offering the perfect view of the large kitchen, bleeding into a family room. Tall glass windows marked the back door along the wall. "But who needs a basement when you have all this space, right?"

222

"Right," I said.

"Come along, I'll show you the rooms."

We followed her down the hallway. There were three doors on each side. The first one on the left was the laundry room, the second one a bathroom, and the third the master suite, which was attached to the bathroom. The three doors on the right all lead into bedrooms, the one at the end of the hall being mine, and the other two for guests when we had visitors.

My walls were grey and my bed was the centre of attention with its large black-rod structure draped in a white canopy.

"Do you like it?" asked Mom. Harper stood beside her. He looked impressed and smiled at me with tenderness in his features, letting me know that if this was all too overwhelming that it would be okay because he was here.

"I do, Mom, you did a great job. The whole house is stunning."

She pulled me into a hug. "I'm so glad you think so. All I want is for you to be happy. Are you happy?"

"Yes," I replied. Because one could still be happy with an aching heart: it was called finding the silver linings of shapes and situations in life. Even through tear-filled eyes one can recognize the sparkle of silver.

"Good," she said, pulling away. "I'll let you two get settled in your rooms, but once you're ready, come down for dinner."

"Thanks, Mom." I heard her socks brush against the carpet as she made her way down the hallway, until they reached the stairs. Then I could hear nothing at all. And the silence was deafening.

Harper still held my bag, so I was forced to turn and look at him. I wished he wasn't so handsome. Maybe then I wouldn't feel so terrified of being around him, and maybe then I wouldn't have gotten myself into the mess of falling.

"You're staring at me," he said.

"I need my bag," I replied.

"Oh, right." He shook his head and offered me the handle. "Here you go. I'll let you get to it."

There was something about being in a bedroom with Harper. The pillows and sheets were too accessible to the burning thoughts that were alight in my mind. They extinguished once he left the room. I exhaled, finally able to breathe again.

## 54

I wasn't moving in until after school, so my drawers looked awfully empty with the few pairs of clothes I had brought with me. The room didn't feel like mine yet because it had yet to be full of me.

The desk next to the window wasn't sprawled with textbooks; it was dotted with novels I had brought to keep me entertained. The vanity had yet to sprout dozens of tiny limbs of makeup brushes because those were at the dorm too.

When I was done unpacking what little I brought, I checked on Harper. He was lying in the middle of the queen-sized bed and he looked like a model lying on his back, atop the white comforter, wearing dark denim. I had to turn away. My clothes must have rustled against the doorframe because he turned to look at me, and I felt his eyes begging for my attention.

I quickly glanced his way. "You ready?" I asked into the air.

"Yep." He hopped off the bed and his shirt got caught on one of his ribs during the motion, his tanned skin all too visible. The burning thoughts started flickering again so I was grateful when his fingers pulled on the hem. It met the waist of his jeans, which didn't help either. I turned around and started walking down the hallway and then down the stairs, into the kitchen where Mom was pulling a pan out of the oven and Dad was mixing a salad.

She rested the tin-foil-covered pan on the stovetop. "Lasagna?" She turned around, smiling. "You don't have any allergies, do you Harper?"

"No, ma'am," he replied. I smirked at his gentlemanly manners and walked over to Dad, analyzing the salad.

"Since when do you cook?" I asked, peering over his shoulder.

His hands clumsily danced with the tongs. "Do these veggies look cooked to you?" he chuckled.

"Nope," I said. "Good point. Want me to take over?"

"Sure," he said.

I took Dad's spot at the counter and sprinkled parmesan cheese into the salad. I then drizzled the vinaigrette dressing across the leaves, tossing the greens back and forth with the tongs until they were glistening with oil. I placed the bowl, tongs sticking out, on the dining table.

Harper walked over to me. "You made that look so easy."

"Don't be fooled," I said. "I can't actually cook."

"Lucky for you, I can," he said.

*Why lucky for me?* I wanted to ask, but as Mom cut the lasagna, she told everyone to sit down. Glasses filled with water and plates with silverware beside them were placed in front of four of the seats. The table sat eight.

When seats were found, Mom placed the pan on top of the hot plates that were laid out. After placing a piece of the dinner on everyone's plate, she sat down too.

"I can't believe Christmas is in four days," said Dad.

"Neither can I," said Mom. "It's all been such a rush, with moving and what not."

"You guys made out okay?" I asked while cutting into my piece of lasagna.

"Yes," said Mom. "We hired movers anyway. All we had to do was unpack."

"Even that in itself is exhausting," said Harper. He took a sip of water.

Mom smiled. "It was." She took a bite of her salad and swallowed. "So, how did you two meet?"

My bites of food started climbing back up my throat. "Ummm…"

"Coffee," said Harper. If my parents knew him better, they would have picked up on how quickly he uttered the word. I did, but it was a good save. "I saw Lora working at the campus cafe and introduced myself."

Mom's smile grew wider. "What a lovely way to meet," she said. "Your cousins will be over tomorrow," said Mom. "They won't be here till late. Uncle Todd and Aunt Sheila will sleep on the pull-out couch upstairs and Elise and Lia will take the other guest room."

"Okay," I said. My little cousins were the cutest, but they weren't so little anymore. Elise was in her first year of high school and Lia was in her last year of grade school. New beginnings and nostalgic ends.

"Your dad and I haven't had a chance to decorate the house," said Mom after taking a sip of water, "which we feel horrible about.

We put up the Christmas tree, but we still have to decorate that too. Would you and Harper mind helping tomorrow?"

Mom eyed the both of us and Harper answered first. "I would love to," he said.

"Me, too," I replied.

"Thank you," said Mom.

When the dishes were cleared and dessert was eaten, it was nearing 9 p.m.

"Your mom and I are going to get ready for bed," said Dad. "Have a good sleep." He hugged me and kissed me on top of my head. Mom kissed me on the cheek.

"Goodnight," I said. They rounded the stairs and climbed their way up. I watched as their hands traced the railing, making out flickers of clothing between the spokes. "I kind of had the same idea," I said, turning to Harper. "I'm tired, are you?"

"I am and I'm not," he said. I tilted my head at him. "I'm an insomniac."

"Oh," I said. "Have you found anything to help with that? I'm sure we have tea somewhere in one of these cupboards. Chamomile is good for calming."

"I'll be fine," he said. "I'll listen to some music or crack open a book."

"You read?" I asked.

"When I find the time it's one of my favourite things," he replied.

"Mine, too," I said. Although, when I found the time, Harper was starting to become one of my favourite people to turn to.

228

"Alright, let's go." I extended my arm toward the staircase, allowing Harper to walk in front of me.

We stopped in the middle of the hallway and leaned against the portion of wall that separated our rooms. Our hair brushed the plaster, our knees almost touching. I wanted to hug him, or at least touch him, but instead I stepped back.

"Well, goodnight, Harper," I said. My fingers clung to the doorframe of my bedroom—the only thing grounding me from running forward and kissing him.

"Goodnight, Lora." He popped into his room and closed the door.

I wanted to open it. I wanted to rush at him and throw my arms around his neck. I want to feel his warmth and breaths.

But instead, I walked into my room too, closing the door behind me.

**55**
———

We had an early start to the day, and I could tell Harper was someone who liked sleeping in, because even by noon he was still rubbing the sleep out of his eyes.

Decorating was successful, but each of us had to tackle a room if we wanted to finish before my cousins arrived. For some areas, like the family room, we worked together because it was too large for one person. We saved the tree for last while nibbling on takeout pizza. Sometime between the first decorations being hung to the star being fitted on the point of the tree, the sun had set and when I looked out the back door the moon was glowing between the clouds. The lake was glow-in-the-dark, a fluorescent blue, and the chops of the ice were bolded in shadows.

I thought I was admiring this view alone. "You want to go out there?" Harper asked. He was standing beside me, his nose almost touching the glass.

"It's probably freezing," I said.

"Well, it is winter," said Harper.

I bounced my shoulder off of his. "I know that, silly. No need to be smart with me."

We both started laughing. "So, do you want to?" he asked.

"Yes," I said. "I very much want to."

"Then let's go."

We walked into the foyer and then into the closet, grabbing our winter gear. Once our hats and gloves were on, we brought our boots to the back door.

Mom poked her head up from adjusting the tree. "We're going to the lake," I told her.

"Okay," she said. "Have fun."

After pulling my boots I pulled my scarf tighter around my neck. "You ready?" I asked.

We looked like Eskimos as we both pulled our hoods up, plumes of fur outlining our faces. "Ready," said Harper.

I unlocked the back door and grabbed hold of the handle. I tugged until there was a space for Harper to walk through, and I followed.

We were silhouettes of the night, shaded with moonlight.

The bitter wind bit through the exposed denim of my jeans and I wished that I was wearing snow pants too. Our breaths were luminescent and glowed like a beacon with the lake.

In a few more steps we reached the edge where the pebbles transitioned to water that was now frozen into ice. The tips of my boots grazed the ice.

"William would have loved this," I said. "He always loved the outdoors more than I. He'd drag me along for hikes and we went camping simply because it made him happy, and if all that made him happy, it made me happy too."

"You've got a big heart, Lora."

My eyes glanced his way, tracing his face, half painted with moonlight, half smudged with shadow. "How so?"

"Even if you don't one hundred percent want to do something, you do it anyway because you think about the other person, not yourself. You're selfless, and it leaves you with a big heart."

I always wished I could see myself from someone else's point of view, to know if my hair was as boring as it looked in the mirror, to see if my nose was too small or if my eyes were too far apart. But it takes a special someone to paint a picture of a person without the hair, the skin and the bones, instead looking under the skin and telling someone about all the colours they're made of.

He called me red.

To me he was sky blue—breathless.

What Harper failed to mention was how my heart grew to be so big: scarring. Layer after layer, pain built its own walls. But life was too short to dwell on the scars inside us, so I grabbed his hand.

"Thank you," I said.

He looked at me and I looked at him. He was the type of person that looked good in any type of lighting, but I especially preferred him in moonlight.

We watched the lake glisten with the moon for a few more moments until I started walking away, tugging his arm. I walked into the trees and I didn't know where I was going until my eyes adjusted to the new amount of darkness.

"There's a path in here," I said to Harper. His eyes were eager so I pulled the both of us farther in.

We were hidden among the darkness and trees, and it was as if the forest was welcoming us—its branches bending our way. We

232

walked in silence, hand-in-hand, until the trail ended. It spits us out onto what I believed was part of the long driveway leading back to the house. My foot was fixed in the groove of a tire track. I broke away from Harper to find another one. I planted my feet in the parallel groove and found Harper standing in the one my feet were just in. He was facing me, but all I saw were his eyes and how they saw me.

My lips became wet, and I realized I had licked them. Butterflies were tickling my throat and I wanted to laugh...or puke. Maybe it was possible to puke butterflies. I would have enjoyed that as a child.

And that was what I felt like right now: a child, a preteen facing her crush for the first time. Because this was the first time— the first time that I didn't care about ruining our perfect and growing friendship. I just wanted to feel his lips.

Harper took a step forward, stamping a single footprint in the untouched snow between the tire tracks, and I wished the groove would swallow me, but I overcame my wish and took a step forward as well—another stamp.

He took another step forward.

I took another step forward.

We inched closer and closer until we were an arm's stretch apart with dozens of stamped footprints circling our feet.

Harper stared at my lips. I stared at his.

Harper leaned in. And I did too.

When I closed my eyes, the whole world fell away and all I could feel was the breaths between mine and Harper's lips. We were close enough to breathe each other's breaths. I was breathing his air, and he was breathing mine. I felt his top lip brush my own when the world became very bright and a honk blared through the night—a car horn—slicing us apart. Even though the headlights reached our feet the vehicle was still far enough away to give us time to run into the forest.

When the vehicle passed and the crunching snow became mute, we met again in the middle of the driveway.

"Those are my cousins," I said. "We should probably head back." I hoped they weren't close enough to make out the details of the scene. It could have looked like we were walking side-by-side.

And I was motioning to do that very thing, heading down the driveway, when Harper grabbed my wrist and spun me around. He was so forceful and close that we smacked into each other. He flung his hand out to meet the back of my head and tugged me to his lips.

And I was lost in the moment.

I didn't know his lips would be so soft and tender. He pulled away but kept his hands on the back of my head.

"I've been wanting to do that for a while now," he whispered.

"I've been wanting you to do that too," I whispered back.

He kissed me again, moving his hands to cup my cheeks.

And it was all wonderful and romantic...

But that was when everything changed.

**56**

———

We didn't kiss anymore after that. Not at my house and not back at campus. It felt like Harper was avoiding me, but I couldn't figure it out. I still went with him to therapy sessions, but we wouldn't talk like we used to. He always had something to do after, but still thanked me for my time. He still texted me but not as much. He seemed distracted.

I tried letting it go and told myself that it was all in my head, but after two weeks, when I got excellent news from one of my teachers, he was the first person I called and it went right to voicemail.

I felt defeated, but I called Mom instead. "Guess what," I said as soon as she picked up.

"What?" she asked. She was already proud of my excitement. Her voice was beaming.

"I got signed!"

"Wait, what?" Mom stuttered. "What do you mean?"

"Mr. Murphy submitted my novel into this contest and whoever won got signed by a publishing company. I won, Mom."

"Oh, Lora, congratulations! I'm so proud of you."

I was smiling so big it hurt my face. "Make sure to tell Dad," I said.

"Oh I will, don't you worry. I have to go now, Lora, I'm waiting on another phone call, but I am so incredibly proud of you. I love you."

"I love you, too," I said.

And when I walked out of the building after class, I leaned against the same wall that Harper and I had leaned on a couple months ago.

And I started crying.

Because it hurt when it felt like someone didn't want you as much as you wanted them.

All I was, was a paper kiss under the moonlight.

It was hard to remind myself that I was more than that.

## 57

I *was* so much more than a kiss, and I was going to tell him so next week, but he didn't show up for therapy.

I texted him, asking him where he was but heard nothing back. I thought that maybe he was still sleeping, so I called his phone instead. Voicemail. I took the last leap of faith and knocked on his dorm door. No one opened it.

This behaviour was unusual, and I thought that maybe he had just gone alone this time. So I took the bus and went to the therapy centre, only to find out he wasn't there either. Dr. Montgomery was just as concerned as I was.

"I'll figure it out," I said.

When I stepped outside to catch the bus back to campus my phone vibrated long and hard. I had an incoming call. I nearly screamed when I saw Harper's name alight on the screen.

"Harper! Harper where are you?" My throat started to close and I knew I was about to cry. "You have me worried sick, I've been looking all…" I stopped my rant because Harper wasn't speaking, he was crying, violently. I'd never heard him cry like that before. "Harper…?"

"Lora…Lora…" he gasped. "I need you."

My voice shook. "Tell me where you are and I'll come running."

He told me.

And I ran.

## 58

I ran until it felt like my lungs were going to explode from contracting and expanding so many times. The street he told me was downtown and led into a damp alley lined with snow.

*Please don't let me relive last year*, I said to myself.

Someone's crumpled body was slouched against the smooth brick wall. It was *his* crumpled body. I only stopped running when I reached him. He looked fine, aside from soaked cheeks and red eyes.

I crouched to the ground so that I was on his level. I looked at his eyes and he looked at me, but he wasn't, just through me.

"Harper? Harper what's wrong?"

"I let everyone down," he croaked. The tears fell silently. The raging sobs on the phone had subsided.

"Harper, you did not. Don't say things like that."

He mustn't have heard me because he was forming words before I finished the sentence. "I let myself down."

He was wearing only a hoodie and started to pull up his right sleeve. My heart clenched.

What looked like a paper cut was drawn across half of his wrist.

"I stopped myself," he said. And he had. He only scratched the surface and the cut had stopped bleeding, but his skin was still angry. Harper was angry too, at himself.

"I told myself," he said, "and I told Dr. Montgomery that this would never happen again, that I would never bring the blade to my skin. But here I am...pathetic...weak..."

"Harper, stop it." I got down on the asphalt beside him and pulled him against me, his head leaning against my chest. "You are none of those things."

"As soon as I did it, I ran. I had to get out of the dorm. I brought the knife with me only to throw it inside a dumpster along the way."

I wanted to ask him what triggered it. I wanted to ask him if I did anything wrong, if he was feeling this way because of me. But those questions were meant for a better time and place, and I just held him as he cried.

But I never got that time and place.

And things didn't get better.

## 59

A week after I turned myself into a human tissue, Harper sent a serious text:

*Harper: Can we meet? I have to talk to you.*

*Okay,* I replied. *Where?*

My nerves grew frenzied. I thought we were fine. I went with him to therapy, made sure he got there, and we even went out for coffee after. All the coffee and kisses were adding up to be superficial.

*Harper: Courtyard. 20 minutes.*

I was confused as to why he wanted to meet in the freezing cold so late in the evening, but once I was bundled and making my way to his lone figure, I understood why. Our words and faces would be cushioned by the night and its wind, but even words said against the wind would hurt, and I'd still be able to make out his features. This felt like goodbye.

And it was.

"Hey," he whispered. As soon as I stood in front of him, he pulled me into a hug and my heart clenched in pain so I backed away.

"Why?" I asked.

"Why?" Harper asked, sounding confused.

"Why hug me Harper? Why kiss me? Why garden me with sweet words and company when all of it doesn't mean shit?"

"Lora…"

"I invite you to *my* home so that you wouldn't have to be alone over the holidays. I stayed for *you*. With *you*. I opened a door in my life and let you walk through it. Everything I've done has been for *you*, except for falling in love…that was *because* of you. Because of who you are. Because of what you say and how you hold yourself. And now I look like a fool because you're walking out. That's what this is, right? You leaving? You saying goodbye? You already gave me that inkling, barely talking to me."

"Lora, this is so much more than that." The moon made the tears that were pooling in the corner of his eyes sparkle.

"Tell me," I begged. "Tell me you didn't fall in love with me too, and I can walk away with a whole heart." I wondered if my face was sparkling too with the streams of tears pouring from my eyes.

He squinted his eyes, trying to get rid of the tears. "Then I guess we'll both be leaving with broken hearts because, Lora, I fell madly and deeply in love with you… I still am…in love with you."

My scream ripped through the night, and I thought about students looking through their dorm windows, but then I thought about life without Harper and let another one loose.

"Lora, shhh." He talked to me through torrents of tears and pulled me close. I couldn't tell whose tears were whose anymore and I didn't care because they were all coming from the same type of feeling: loss.

A few months ago I was getting lost in him.

But now we were losing each other…

…and my whole damn world was falling apart.

"It has to be this way," said Harper. His words slipped down the strands of my hair and into my ears. It hurt.

"I can't be in your life Lora, I'm no good for you." His lips brushed my left temple. "I'm not even good for myself."

I unfolded myself from his arms and backed away. "I can't make you stay," I croaked, "but I'll beg on my hands and knees if that's what it takes to make you live this life with me."

I gulped then shouted, "There's nothing I want more than to be yours, Harper."

My words slapped him across his face and his features scrunched in pain. "It just can't be this way, I'm sorry," he said.

"If you're worried about being broken and all the broken pieces inside you, then stop, because I don't care, Harper. I'm broken too—we all are in some sort of way." I raised my hands, motioning to either side of me, around me. I looked at the sky and felt tears roll down the sides of my jaw. "The whole universe is made of particles that separate and expand, it's just a scientific way of saying they break apart. The whole universe is breaking around us, but we don't have to."

I scanned his face, searching for some type of hope that this may last. Coming up short hurts. "Goodbye, Lora."

I watched his face collapse one last time before he turned around and walked away.

**60**
———

*2013*

What happened that night tore me up for a long time, but eventually, I learned to sew the pieces back into place. I took all the unread texts and voicemail calls and wove them into a scarf that I tied tight around my heart, keeping it warm from the coldness of sadness. But the moments were still there, a reminder of what I went through and the strength it took to get over it.

My parents never asked about Harper when I didn't bring him home for a second time, and I graduated from university. When I walked across the stage, a part of me wished to see his brown curls and dopey smile, but all I saw was a sea of strangers and two faces of love—my parents.

I landed an editing position at a publishing house in Toronto and moved into an apartment with Deirdre. It was easier to split rent when you were just starting your career.

The times I traveled to and from work, I wondered how Harper was doing. I wondered if he was still in the city, if he had graduated, if he too was using transit to get to work. Did he have a job? A lot could have happened in five years.

I was still thinking about this as I walked into the bookstore and saw piles of my books already waiting for me, sitting on top of a table. The owner walked over to me, shaking my hand.

"It's so nice to meet you and thank you so much for coming here."

"Of course," I said. "It's my pleasure."

He showed me where I could put my purse and showed me where I could sit. He led me to a tall chair in front of a microphone and when I sat down, I was overwhelmed by the number of people who had come to hear me speak, to get their books signed. The owner had to ask the employees to get more chairs from storage, as some were standing.

My deal went smoothly with the publishing company, and in four years my book hit the shelves—a romance story. I had to finish writing the end of the novel. I had to finish school and then the process began. One year later, I was still attending book signings.

The owner let me know when I could begin. I introduced myself and explained how I got into writing and my journey as an author, how this was my first book and I was grateful for all the support. I read two chapters, answered people's questions, and then they lined up to get books signed.

I stayed a half-hour later after the event, talking with the employees and the owner about their lives, when a tuft of brown curls whipped by the window. The bell above the door rang and in walked Harper Lee Engels.

He didn't look much different. Maybe he was a little taller and he had some stubble, but to me, he looked like the same Harper from five years ago.

The one who rode the city buses with me.

The one who pulled me close for the first time in a laundromat.

The one who made me give up on love.

It was him, and he was carrying a copy of my book in his hand. He raked his hand through his hair. "Shoot, I missed it didn't I?" He talked to the owner, unable to look at me.

"I'm afraid so sir, but lucky for you, the author is still here to sign your copy."

And then, he did look at me, and the scarf I had tied so tightly around my heart started to loosen. I walked over to the table where the stacks of books had once been and grabbed my pen from my purse. I sat in the chair and Harper stood across from me at the other side of the table. I clicked the pen, opening the book to the cover page, not knowing what to write.

"I was impressed to see you wrote a book," he said. His voice was trembling. "But I was even more impressed when I read it. I never knew what a brilliant writer you are."

"You never stuck around to find out," I replied, staring at him. He looked away and I brought the black pen to the paper, writing:

*This is the love story you never gave me. - Lora*

I clicked my pen again and put it back in my purse. I slid the book back to Harper and when he read the message, I found it hard not to laugh. He was sweating with guilt.

"Ah, I see," he said. "Do you mind if I take you out for coffee? There's a great cafe just around the corner."

"I know the place," I said. "And it's not that great. Also, I do mind. I have somewhere to be."

I didn't wait for his response. I picked up my purse, thanked the owner, and left the store.

**61**

———

I didn't have anywhere to be on a Saturday, but I didn't want to go anywhere in the company of Harper. I was 25 and too old to play games.

I took a streetcar home and was happy to find Deirdre on the couch watching a movie.

"How did it go?" she asked, looking at the screen. "Marvelous as always?" Then she looked at me and frowned. "You look beat."

I threw my purse on the bench at the entrance. "You *will not* believe who came by 30 minutes late," I spat, flailing my arms, walking back and forth.

Deirdre paused the movie and removed her feet from the coffee table to face me. "Who?"

"Harper," I said.

She rushed to my side and hugged me. That's when I started crying.

I cried all night because I hadn't cried about it in the last three years, but seeing him ripped off the bandage I had glued over the crack in my heart and it hurt all over again.

## 62

———

I didn't realize having the same phone number all my life could cause such pain until a random number texted me:

*Unknown: Hi, Lora?*

*Who's this?* I responded right away. I was on lunch break.

*Unknown: It's Harper.*

Immediately, I deleted the message, wrapped up my lunch, and walked back to my desk to work on a manuscript.

I didn't lift my head until the clock on my computer said 5 p.m. When I checked my phone, I had three missed calls, all from Harper. With the last one he left a voicemail.

I didn't listen to his message until midnight. Even though I showered and was wrapped in thick blankets, cozied in my bed, it was still difficult to plug in the passcode to my voicemail and bring the phone to my ear. It was even more difficult to listen to the whole message.

With every sorry and regret I heard in his voice I wanted to hit the end button, but I didn't. Because even though hearing his voice hurt, it also soothed an aching part of me that still longed to be his. He was the only boy I ever loved. I tried seeing other people, but it just never worked out. They were too weird, or they talked about themselves too much.

When the voicemail ended, I leaned against my pillows and shut off the lamp.

I didn't cry, but I was weighed down by a heavy heart.

## 63

------

Harper texted me for two weeks in a row. I didn't answer.

So, he texted me another two weeks, always asking about coffee, and every time I said no.

But after a month, I was getting fed up and said yes.

His victory ended up being my victory too.

He chose a coffee shop down the street from my apartment and the awkwardness across the table was pushed away with small talk. With real talk came tension.

He told me he was an art teacher and owned his own studio. He told me he continued with therapy and still goes once a month, to this day. He told me he's cleaned himself up, mentally—that the bad days only happen on a bi-monthly basis instead of everyday. I told him that was a great thing.

"I also offer therapy classes," he said.

"Therapy?"

"For me, especially growing up, art was the only way I could express myself. So, every Wednesday night, I invite people who suffer from mental illness, and those who don't if they just want to paint, to come to the studio and paint about how they're feeling."

"Wow," I said. I couldn't help but smile. "That's amazing."

"Thank you," he said. "I see you've been successful as well, with your book and all."

"Yes," I said. "I'm also an editor at a publishing house."

"You keep impressing me more and more, Lora."

I didn't say anything, just took a sip of coffee. He spun his cup in a circle between his fingers and I could sense he felt as uneasy as I did.

"Why did you ask me out for coffee, Harper? Why did you persist even when I said no?"

"Because, Lora," he looked at his cup as he continued to spin it, around and around and around. "Five years ago...I messed up."

"You're kidding me," I said. I raised my voice without meaning to and the people sitting at tables around us swiveled their heads in our direction, waiting to see if I'd do so again. I wanted to get up. I wanted to walk down the street, as far away as possible from this situation, as far as possible from Harper.

"Why, Harper? Why now? I've already normalized my life without you."

"I don't know, Lora. I know it's horrible timing, and I wish the me five years ago never let you go. I've regretted it ever since. You were the best thing in my life."

I took a sip of coffee and smacked the cup against the table. It was loud enough for a few heads to turn our way again. "And, what? Do you expect me to welcome you with open arms as if what happened five years ago never happened?"

"Of course not, Lora. To expect that of you would be absolutely foolish. I'm just telling you how I feel out of the slightest hope that somewhere inside, you still feel the same. That you might take me back."

I drank the coffee until the cup was empty and got up to throw it out. When I walked back to the table, I took my purse from where it was hanging on the chair and slid it onto my shoulder.

"Have a nice life, Harper."

I stormed out of the cafe because his slight ounce of hope was correct, and I didn't want it to be.

**64**

—

It didn't matter how cruelly I had treated Harper: he still didn't give up. It was a Monday night, and I was venting to Deirdre over wine and sautéed dumplings.

"He's relentless," I said, taking a sip of wine. I placed the cup in front of me, next to the bowl, and took a seat. "I don't think he'll ever give up, and that's scary as hell."

Deirdre talked around a bite. "You haven't told him to get gone?"

"I have," I said. "Many times, too many times! I literally up and left him the other day over coffee and he's still texting me, still calling every day." I picked up the pair of chopsticks that laid next to the bowl and plopped a dumpling in my mouth, not caring about the corner sticking out between my lips.

"If you've really had enough, why not just block his number?"

I had thought about this but decided against it. "Because I can't bring myself to do that," I told Deirdre. "I've missed him for five years and suddenly he just pops back into my life? There has to be a reason, right?"

She takes a sip of wine. "Maybe you two were meant to be."

"What?" That was the last thing I expected to hear coming out of Deirdre's mouth.

"I mean it, Lora. If I were in your shoes and a guy came back for me after five years of parting ways, I'd take him back. If that's not saying he cares, I don't know what does."

I took another swig of wine, a bigger one this time, thinking it would make it easier to swallow the truth.

When we finished the dumplings and bottle of wine I crawled into bed with my phone and texted Harper:

*When can I see you next?*

I was almost done with my lunch break when Harper replied to my text from last night.

*Harper: What's your work address?*

I stopped chewing my sandwich mid-bite. "Why?" I texted back.

*Harper: I would just like to know.*

I quickly punched in the name of the street, followed by the three digits and pressed send.

*Harper: Thank you.*

I finished my lunch and walked back to my desk. I leaned back in my chair and opened my email. Harper was up to something. I just didn't know what it was yet.

I had an hour left of work when the office secretary walked over to my desk, handing me a bouquet of roses.

"This came for you, Lora." She smiled at me. "You're a very lucky woman."

"Thank you," I said

When she walked away, I checked the card that was attached to the colourful foil, wrapped around the stems. It read:

*To Lora,*

*With love.*

*- Harper*

I reread the message several times, unsure of his words. *With love* could mean a lot of things, and I didn't want my guess to be

256

wrong. Because even when I was certain about falling in love with Harper, that came back and bit me in the ass.

And now he was here. Sending flowers.

I didn't know if Harper or I could undo past pains. Would it be worth it to be together, or would it be too hard?

But Dad told me the hardest things in life are the most worth it. You just have to work for it.

**66**

———

So that was what we did. We worked at it.

I started spending my lunch breaks with him. He'd meet me at my building and take me to a deli or cuisine, somewhere that was sit-down and cute, yet quick. I never paid, not once. I didn't complain this time.

Eventually, lunches turned into dinners. Every Friday was date night. Sometimes he'd take me to a fancy restaurant and other times to see a movie. Once a week turned into twice a week and before I knew it, I was spending weekends at his apartment. He cooked breakfast and would bring it to me on a tray to eat in bed.

Half a year went by filled with these familiar routines and we talked about getting our own place together. One morning, when Harper was reading the paper, he saw listings for some subdivision homes in the Etobicoke area. I pointed to one with slate blue paneling.

"That one, that one looks nice," I said. "Not too big, not too small. Just right."

That same morning, he demanded that I get out of bed early and head to the bookstore with him. I couldn't say no because no one in their right mind would refuse to surround themselves with books, especially with the one they love.

It was an hour bus ride and then thirty minutes on the subway, but the lengthy transit didn't bother me with Harper by my side.

Eventually we arrived at the Eaton Centre, a ginormous mall that housed my most favourite Indigo store, with two levels and a spiral staircase.

I've walked into bookstores hundreds of times in my life and the scent of paper and ink never got old. I always took a minute to stand in one spot, close my eyes, and breathe in all the scents that were mixed into the atmosphere. Aside from pages, I also smelled coffee. Harper held my hand and led me to my favourite section: Teen Fiction. Even though I was 25 years old, I was a sucker for young adult stories. I'd tell Harper these kinds of books kept me young and he'd just laugh at me.

My eyes were scanning the section that held Sarah Dessen's novels, and I was pulling out *Along for The Ride* when I noticed Harper was no longer beside me. His warmth had vanished. I spun around, scouring the area, until I looked down, right in front of me, and that was when I saw him...

He was down on one knee holding a black, patented box with a tiny diamond sticking out.

My hands flew to my mouth, pushing back the surprise that wanted to be let loose. Instead it came out in tears.

"Harper..."

I stared into his eyes and at the ring. I couldn't breathe. I was hyperventilating into my hand.

"Lora," he said. "I know I'm not perfect, in fact, I've made some pretty shitty mistakes that I'll be making up to you for the rest of my life. But I can only do that if you want to spend the rest of your life with me. You're my best friend and I couldn't imagine a life without you, because I already had a portion of one without, and it was unbearable." A tear slipped from his right eye. "Lora, will you do me the honour of being my wife?"

It was already an intense moment but I became even more emotional when the book shoppers around us started to flock, viewing the proposal.

"Yes, Harper, yes, of course!"

And now I was full out crying, and I was afraid that when he slipped the ring on my left ring finger that it would get stuck. But it was a perfect fit. He pulled me close like he did years ago, one chilly night, standing on my driveway. And he kissed me the same way too: slow and tender. If I wasn't leaning into him and if Harper didn't have his arms around me, I would have collapsed to the floor.

People started to dissipate, letting us share our intimate moment between the two of us, and I was grateful because I wanted him all to myself.

## 67

---

*2018*

Just thinking about it makes my face hurt like it did that day, from smiling so much and so wide.

We ended up buying the slate blue, paneled house and my parents helped us move in. This was, of course, after having a small wedding with my family and both of our groups of friends. We didn't want to wait.

Harper and I maintained a healthy marriage, always making time for each other outside of our careers. We never had children but adopted two cats from the shelter: Molly and Moe. They were around six years old and when I came home with them one day, Harper threw a fit.

"They're middle-aged," I said. "No one wants a cat older than three. They never would have gotten adopted if it weren't for me."

He became best friends with the animals and often cuddled them at night instead of me.

Even though we laughed more than we fought, we still had our difficulties, especially on Harper's bad days. Sometimes I'd call in sick to work at home, to stay with him and keep him company, because even though he told me not to, I didn't want him to be alone.

Sometimes we'd do just that—stay home—and other times we'd go to the studio and I'd set up two canvases, one for him and one for me, and we'd paint until the sun set.

I *pretended* like I knew what I was doing.

Harper *actually* knew what he was doing.

And every time he'd paint something more beautiful than the last, and I didn't know how it was possible.

Along with painting, he attended therapy every month. He said he liked going and that he always felt better after, more refreshed.

"You should come to one of my art therapy sessions," he told me one day.

"Okay," I said.

So off we went together one Wednesday evening. I sat in the back and watched how Harper interacted with kids—effortless. He'd make them laugh and if someone was crying, he knew how to make them smile through the tears. Even though he and I were great with children, we agreed that we were too scared to have our own and were content with one another.

One of the boys reminded me of him. He looked like he was about 17, with the same brown, unruly hair. But it was the way he painted that I found the most striking resemblance. He took an emotion and made a character. He gave it a face that possessed jagged beauty. He was painting something blue, with darker shades for outlines. It looked like sadness.

When we got home that night and tucked into bed, I told him, "What you do is amazing. You touch so many people's lives. You should be proud of yourself."

He shrugged his shoulders. "I guess. Sometimes it doesn't feel like enough."

His words worried me. "Am I enough, Harper?"

"You're more than enough, Lora, way more."

But I wasn't.

**68**

---

*October 1st, 2023*

*Dear Lora,*

*You were always the brightest light in my life, and I didn't know how sweet you'd be when I first saw you sitting next to me in the hospital room. I still think that's when I knew I'd fall in love with you.*

*I was always grateful that you had found me, but some days, even in our thirties, I wish you hadn't, because I'm nothing but a burden. A weight.*

*I knew I could never push away my love for you, and I wanted you more than anything, so I came back.*

*Writing this, I wish I hadn't, because it would have saved you from a lot of pain.*

*I stopped attending therapy. I didn't want to tell you because I didn't want to upset you. While you were at work in the mornings, I'd lay in bed and cry. I didn't want you to know that I was still the same broken pile of a person I was 15 years ago. I tried to hide it from you because all I ever wanted to do was make you happy. I could hide it on the outside, but on the inside is where depression ran wild, and I couldn't hide from myself.*

*I said I wanted you more than anything, but sometimes, I wanted something else more, and it kept pressing on me until I gave in.*

*I don't think I'm going to heaven, but I don't think I'll go to hell. Maybe there's an in-between window where I can still watch you living your life with writing books and reading them.*

*I hope, on hands and knees, that there is a window, because not being able to see you will be the most painful of things, but I know my life would be more painful if I remained alive.*

*I always told you, you deserved better, Lora.*

*This is me giving it to you.*

*Love always,*

*H*

## 69

*October 5, 2023*

I won't say how he did it, out of respect for the dead—that was their story to tell, and I never felt comfortable talking to people about it. A part of my brain believed that if I didn't talk about it at all, then it didn't happen at all, but my nightmares always reminded me.

I once told myself that my whole world was falling apart— that was when Harper walked out of my life.

But that was temporary.

This was permanent.

And I was a black hole, disappearing inside myself until I was nonexistent. Or so it felt.

My parents sat beside me, one on either side, as if placing me between two sturdy objects could keep me standing. There was music in the background but all I saw was Harper's face flashing from olive to white, from olive to white. Alive to dead.

My fingers tightened around the paper in my hand and when I looked down, a few tears splattered the written words, smearing the ink. When I looked up, rays of sun shone through the stained-glass window, reflecting in blues and purples. The light reached the podium where I was ushered to stand and talk into a tiny microphone.

The tears had dried and my skin felt tight in the salty casing they left. I cleared my throat.

"Harper's illness did not define him." My throat tightened and I feared I wouldn't be able to continue, but if Harper were here, he'd tell me I could. "He was so much more than that."

My hands shook the paper as I continued. "Harper was a brilliant student, an artist. Harper was a loving boyfriend, fiancé, and husband. Harper was a committed teacher.

"He was the person you'd want to call late at night when you felt sad. He was the person who would barbecue the best steaks and brew the best coffee. He was the person who picked up the newspaper for our neighbors and brought it to their door. He was the person who'd give the elderly, children and moms his seat on transit. He was the person who'd paint such beautiful pictures they'd make you cry."

A shiver crept over my body and I trembled. My voice shook. "He was the first and only person I fell in love with. He was the person I started a life with and hoped to end it with as well, but we can never predict the future."

I cleared my throat again. "If your loved ones suffer from mental illness, hold them close and appreciate them for their flaws and their quirks. Because people are more than their bad days. If all they can do is cry that day then sit beside them. Hand them tissues. And if they're laughing that day? Laugh with them too, give them a hug. Many of us don't understand depression and will never understand the illness. I still don't fully, because the complexities of it are more than our minds can understand.

"I didn't have to understand Harper's depression to love him. He was more than that. He was my moment-by-moment adventure, and I will cherish every single moment I had with him."

Bursts of sobs echoed among the people congregated, but I kept even breathing until I sat back down, until it was time to leave the church and walk outside.

It looked weird to see Harper hovering above a hole in the ground. I wanted to fit my body under it to cushion his fall.

I watched as flowers were placed on the casket.

When it came my turn, I walked alone. I placed a red rose and an envelope on top of the pile. Some last words.

From that day, I continued to love him.

*Dear Harper,*

*To the one I love, please wait for me wherever you are, so that one day we can be together again, because a close friend once told me that we were meant to be. Maybe I'll go camping sometime and find you among the stars—you'll spot me looking your way, and I'll know the star that shines the brightest will be you. And I'll know the next brightest star will be William, standing beside you.*

*Loving you without you,*
*Lora*

**THE END**

THANK YOU FOR READING *MORE THAN US*.

We hope you enjoyed exploring Harper and Lora's story.

Please consider posting a rating or review to sites like Goodreads and Amazon.

Reviews are the lifeblood of authors and help more readers like you find their new favorite books.

## About the Author

**Ryan Jones** is a writer and editor residing in Southwestern Ontario. She loves a good book, a good cup of tea and snuggles from her cats. She strives to find the silver lining of every situation in life and hopes to inspire and comfort people through writing literature.

Find her online at the following locations:

Website: www.bibliovirgo.com

Twitter: @bibliovirgo_

Instagram: bibliovirgo